# THE POISON BELT AND OTHER STORIES

These lively, varied and thought-provoking science-fiction stories (from the era of Jules Verne and H. G. Wells) are linked by their imposing central character, the pugnaciously adventurous and outrageous Professor Challenger. *The Poison Belt* presents an eerie doomsday scenario, while in *The Disintegration Machine* the deadliest invention ever created is offered up for sale to the highest bidder. Finally, in *When the World Screamed*, the planet responds violently to an experimental incursion . . .

*Books by Sir Arthur Conan Doyle*
*Published by The House of Ulverscroft:*

A STUDY IN SCARLET
THE SIGN OF FOUR
THE ADVENTURES OF
SHERLOCK HOLMES
MEMOIRS OF SHERLOCK HOLMES
THE RETURN OF SHERLOCK HOLMES
THE HOUND OF THE BASKERVILLES
THE VALLEY OF FEAR
HIS LAST BOW
THE CASEBOOK OF SHERLOCK HOLMES
THE EXPLOITS OF BRIGADIER GERARD
THE ADVENTURES OF GERARD
THE LOST WORLD

SIR ARTHUR CONAN DOYLE

# THE POISON BELT

## AND OTHER STORIES

*Complete and Unabridged*

# ULVERSCROFT
*Leicester*

*The Poison Belt* first published
in Great Britain in 1913
*The Disintegration Machine* first published
in Great Britain in 1929
*When the World Screamed* first published
in Great Britain in 1928


This Large Print Edition
published 2014


The moral right of the author has been asserted

*A catalogue record for this book is available
from the British Library.*


ISBN 978–1–4448–2037–9


Published by
F. A. Thorpe (Publishing)
Anstey, Leicestershire

Set by Words & Graphics Ltd.
Anstey, Leicestershire
Printed and bound in Great Britain by
T. J. International Ltd., Padstow, Cornwall

This book is printed on acid-free paper

# SPECIAL MESSAGE TO READERS

## THE ULVERSCROFT FOUNDATION
**(registered UK charity number 264873)**
was established in 1972 to provide funds for
research, diagnosis and treatment of eye diseases.
Examples of major projects funded by
the Ulverscroft Foundation are:-

- The Children's Eye Unit at Moorfields Eye Hospital, London
- The Ulverscroft Children's Eye Unit at Great Ormond Street Hospital for Sick Children
- Funding research into eye diseases and treatment at the Department of Ophthalmology, University of Leicester
- The Ulverscroft Vision Research Group, Institute of Child Health
- Twin operating theatres at the Western Ophthalmic Hospital, London
- The Chair of Ophthalmology at the Royal Australian College of Ophthalmologists

You can help further the work of the Foundation
by making a donation or leaving a legacy.
Every contribution is gratefully received. If you
would like to help support the Foundation or
require further information, please contact:

**THE ULVERSCROFT FOUNDATION**
**The Green, Bradgate Road, Anstey**
**Leicester LE7 7FU, England**
**Tel: (0116) 236 4325**

website: ft.com

Sir Arthur Conan Doyle was born in Edinburgh, Scotland, in 1859. He studied medicine at the University of Edinburgh, where he met Dr. Joseph Bell, upon whose habits and abilities in the sphere of deductive reasoning Doyle would later base his most famous creation, Sherlock Holmes. After working for a time as a ship's doctor, he established his own medical practice near Portsmouth, where the lack of patients led to him spending his time working on his Holmesian stories — the enormous success of which enabled him to give up the practice and devote his time to writing. During the Boer War, Doyle served as volunteer doctor in the Langman Field Hospital, Bloemfontein. A fervent advocate of justice, he was also a campaigner for reform of the Congo Free State; domestically, he personally investigated two closed criminal cases, which led to both of the accused being exonerated of the crimes. A prolific author — whose works included science fiction, crime fiction, historical novels, poetry, and political treatises — he died in 1930.

# Contents

# Contents

## THE CONJURING ARTS

## THE SPIRITUALISTIC MEDIUM

## THE ESCAPE MAGICIAN

# THE POISON BELT

# 1

## The Blurring of the Lines

It is imperative that now at once, while these stupendous events are still clear in my mind, I should set them down with that exactness of detail which time may blur. But even as I do so, I am overwhelmed by the wonder of the fact that it should be our little group of the 'Lost World' — Professor Challenger, Professor Summerlee, Lord John Roxton, and myself — who have passed through this amazing experience.

When, some years ago, I chronicled in the *Daily Gazette* our epoch-making journey in South America, I little thought that it should ever fall to my lot to tell an even stranger personal experience, one which is unique in all human annals, and must stand out in the records of history as a great peak among the humble foothills which surround it. The event itself will always be marvellous, but the circumstances that we four were together at the time of this extraordinary episode came about in a most natural and, indeed, inevitable fashion. I will explain the events which led up to it as shortly and as clearly as I can, though I am well aware that the fuller the detail upon such a subject the more welcome it will be to the reader, for the public curiosity has been and still is insatiable.

It was upon Friday, the twenty-seventh of August — a date for ever memorable in the history of the world — that I went down to the office of my paper and asked for three days' leave of absence from Mr McArdle, who still presided over our news department. The good old Scotchman shook his head, scratched his dwindling fringe of ruddy fluff, and finally put his reluctance into words.

'I was thinking, Mr Malone, that we could employ you to advantage these days. I was thinking there was a story that you are the only man that could handle as it should be handled.'

'I am sorry for that,' said I, trying to hide my disappointment. 'Of course if I am needed, there is an end of the matter. But the engagement was important and intimate. If I could be spared — '

'Well, I don't see that you can.'

It was bitter, but I had to put the best face I could upon it. After all, it was my own fault, for I should have known by this time that a journalist has no right to make plans of his own.

4

'Then I'll think no more of it,' said I, with as much cheerfulness as I could assume at so short a notice. 'What was it that you wanted me to do?'

'Well, it was just to interview that deevil of a man down at Rotherfield.'

'You don't mean Professor Challenger?' I cried.

'Aye, it's just him that I do mean. He ran young Alec Simpson, of the *Courier*, a mile down the high road last week by the collar of his coat and the slack of his breeches. You'll have read of it, likely, in the police report. Our boys would as soon interview a loose alligator in the Zoo. But you could do it, I'm thinking — an old friend like you.'

'Why,' said I, greatly relieved, 'this makes it all easy. It so happens that it was to visit Professor Challenger at Rotherfield that I was asking for leave of absence. The fact is, that it is the anniversary of our main adventure on the plateau three years ago, and he has asked our whole party down to his house to see him and celebrate the occasion.'

'Capital!' cried McArdle, rubbing his hands and beaming through his glasses. 'Then you will be able to get his opeenions out of him. In any other man I would say it was all moonshine, but the fellow has made good once, and who knows but he may again!'

'Get what out of him?' I asked. 'What has he been doing?'

'Haven't you seen his letter on 'Scientific Possibeelities' in today's *Times*?'

'No.'

McArdle dived down and picked a copy from the floor.

'Read it aloud,' said he, indicating a column with his finger. 'I'd be glad to hear it again, for I am not sure now that I have the man's meaning clear in my head.'

This was the letter which I read to the news editor of the *Gazette*:

'*Scientific Possibilities*

'Sir — I have read with amusement, not wholly unmixed with some less complimentary emotion, the complacent and wholly fatuous letter of James Wilson MacPhail, which has lately appeared in your columns upon the subject of the blurring of Frauenhofer's lines in the spectra both of the planets and of the fixed stars. He dismisses the matter as of no significance. To a wider intelligence it may well seem of very great possible importance — so great as to involve the ultimate welfare of every man, woman, and child upon this planet. I can hardly hope, by the use of scientific language, to convey any sense of my meaning to those ineffectual people who gather their ideas from the columns of a daily newspaper. I will endeavour, therefore, to condescend to their limitation, and to indicate the situation by the use of a homely analogy which will be within the limits of the intelligence of your readers.'

'Man, he's a wonder — a living wonder!' said McArdle, shaking his head reflectively. 'He'd put up the feathers of a sucking-dove and set up a riot in a Quaker's meeting. No wonder he has made London too hot for him. It's a peety, Mr Malone, for it's a grand brain! Well, let's have the analogy.'

'We will suppose [I read] that a small bundle of connected corks was launched in a sluggish current upon a voyage across the Atlantic. The corks drift slowly on from day to day with the same conditions all round them. If the corks were sentient we could imagine that they would consider these conditions to be permanent and assured. But we, with our superior knowledge, know that many things might happen to surprise the corks. They might possibly float up

7

against a ship, or a sleeping whale, or become entangled in seaweed. In any case, their voyage would probably end by their being thrown up on the rocky coast of Labrador. But what could they know of all this while they drifted so gently day by day in what they thought was a limitless and homogeneous ocean?

'Your readers will possibly comprehend that the Atlantic, in this parable, stands for the mighty ocean of ether through which we drift, and that the bunch of corks represents the little and obscure planetary system to which we belong. A third-rate sun, with its rag-tag and bobtail of insignificant satellites, we float under the same daily conditions towards some unknown end, some squalid catastrophe which will overwhelm us at the ultimate confines of space, where we are swept over an etheric Niagara, or dashed upon some unthinkable Labrador. I see no room here for the shallow and ignorant optimism of your correspondent, Mr James Wilson MacPhail, but many reasons why we should watch with a very close and interested attention every indication of change in those cosmic surroundings upon which our own ultimate fate may depend.'

'Man, he'd have made a grand meenister,' said McArdle. 'It just booms like an organ. Let's get down to what it is that's troubling him.'

'The general blurring and shifting of Frauenhofer's lines of the spectrum point, in my opinion, to a widespread cosmic change of a subtle and singular character. Light from a planet is the reflected light of the sun. Light from a star is a self-produced light. But the spectra both from planets and stars have, in this instance, all undergone the same change. Is it, then, a change in those planets and stars? To me such an idea is inconceivable. What common change could simultaneously come upon them all? Is it a change in our own atmosphere? It is possible, but in the highest degree improbable, since we see no signs of it around us, and chemical analysis has failed to reveal it. What, then, is the third possibility? That it may be a change in the conducting medium, in that infinitely fine ether which extends from star to star and pervades the whole universe. Deep in that ocean we are floating upon a slow current. Might that current not drift us into belts of ether which are novel and have properties of which we have never con-ceived? There is a change somewhere. This

9

cosmic disturbance of the spectrum proves it. It may be a good change. It may be an evil one. It may be a neutral one. We do not know. Shallow observers may treat the matter as one which can be disregarded, but one who like myself is possessed of the deeper intelligence of the true philosopher will understand that the possibilities of the universe are incalculable and that the wisest man is he who holds himself ready for the unexpected. To take an obvious example, who would undertake to say that the mysterious and universal outbreak of illness, recorded in your columns this very morning as having broken out among the indigenous races of Sumatra, has no connection with some cosmic change to which they may respond more quickly than the more complex peoples of Europe? I throw out the idea for what it is worth. To assert it is, in the present stage, as unprofitable as to deny it, but it is an unimaginative numskull who is too dense to perceive that it is well within the bounds of scientific possibility.

'Yours faithfully,
   'GEORGE EDWARD CHALLENGER
    '*The Briars, Rotherfield*'

'It's a fine, steemulating letter,' said McArdle, thoughtfully, fitting a cigarette into the long glass tube which he used as a holder. 'What's your opeenion of it, Mr Malone?'

I had to confess my total and humiliating ignorance of the subject at issue. What, for example, were Frauenhofer's lines? McArdle had just been studying the matter with the aid of our tame scientist at the office, and he picked from his desk two of those many-coloured spectral bands which bear a general resemblance to the hat-ribbons of some young and ambitious cricket club. He pointed out to me that there were certain black lines which formed crossbars upon the series of brilliant colours extending from the red at one end, through gradations of orange, yellow, green, blue, and indigo, to the violet at the other.

'Those dark bands are Frauenhofer's lines,' said he. 'The colours are just light itself. Every light, if you can split it up with a prism, gives the same colours. They tell us nothing. It is the lines that count, because they vary according to what it may be that produces the light. It is these lines that have been blurred instead of clear this last week, and all the astronomers have been quarrelling over the reason. Here's a photograph of the blurred lines for our issue tomorrow. The public have taken no interest in the matter up to now, but this letter of Challenger's in *The Times* will make them wake up, I'm thinking.'

'And this about Sumatra?'

'Well, it's a long cry from a blurred line in a spectrum to a sick nigger in Sumatra. And yet the chief has shown us once before that he knows what he's talking about. There is some queer illness down yonder, that's beyond all doubt, and today there's a cable just come in from Singapore that the lighthouses are out of action in the Straits of Sunda, and two ships on the beach in consequence. Anyhow, it's good enough for you to interview Challenger upon. If you get anything definite, let us have a column by Monday.'

I was coming out from the news editor's room, turning over my new mission in my mind, when I heard my name called from the waiting-room below. It was a telegraph-boy with a wire which had been forwarded from my lodgings at Streatham. The message was from the very man we had been discussing, and ran thus: 'Malone, 17 Hill Street, Streatham. Bring oxygen. CHALLENGER.'

'Bring oxygen!' The Professor, as I remembered him, had an elephantine sense of humour capable of the most clumsy and unwieldy gambollings. Was this one of those jokes which used to reduce him to uproarious laughter, when his eyes would disappear, and he was all gaping mouth and wagging beard, supremely indifferent to the gravity of all around him? I turned the words over, but could make nothing even remotely jocose out of them. Then surely it was a concise order — though a very strange one. He was the last man in the world whose deliberate command I should care to disobey. Possibly some chemical experiment was afoot; possibly — Well, it was no business of mine to speculate upon why he wanted it. I must get it. There was nearly an hour before I should catch the train at Victoria. I took a taxi, and having ascertained the address from the telephone book, I made for the Oxygen Tube Supply Company in Oxford Street.

As I alighted on the pavement at my destination, two youths emerged from the door of the establishment carrying an iron cylinder, which, with some trouble, they hoisted into a waiting motorcar. An elderly man was at their heels scolding and directing in a creaky, sardonic voice. He turned towards me. There was no mistaking those austere features and that goatee beard. It was my old cross-grained companion, Professor Summerlee.

'What!' he cried. 'Don't tell me that you have had one of these preposterous telegrams for oxygen?'

I exhibited it.

'Well, well! I have had one, too, and, as you see, very much against the grain, I have acted upon it. Our good friend is as impossible as ever. The need for oxygen could not have been so urgent that he must desert the usual means of supply and encroach upon the time of those who are really busier than himself. Why could he not order it direct?'

I could only suggest that he probably wanted it at once.

'Or thought he did, which is quite another matter. But it is superfluous now for you to purchase any, since I have this considerable supply.'

'Still, for some reason he seems to wish that I should bring oxygen too. It will be safer to do exactly what he tells me.'

Accordingly, in spite of many grumbles and remonstrances from Summerlee, I ordered an additional tube, which was placed with the other in his motorcar, for he had offered me a lift to Victoria.

I turned away to pay off my taxi, the driver of which was very cantankerous and abusive over his fare. As I came back to Professor Summerlee, he was having a furious altercation with the men who had carried down the oxygen, his little white goat's beard jerking with indignation. One of the fellows called him, I remember, 'a silly old bleached cockatoo,' which so enraged his chauffeur that he bounded out of his seat to take the part of his insulted master, and it was all we could do to prevent a riot in the street.

These little things may seem trivial to relate, and passed as mere incidents at the time. It is only now, as I look back, that I see their relation to the whole story which I have to unfold.

The chauffeur must, as it seemed to me, have been a novice or else have lost his nerve in this disturbance, for he drove vilely on the way to the station. Twice we nearly had collisions with other equally erratic vehicles, and I remember remarking to Summerlee that the standard of driving in London had very much declined. Once we brushed the very edge of a great crowd which was watching a fight at the corner of the Mall. The people, who were much excited, raised cries of anger at the clumsy driving, and one fellow sprang upon the step and waved a stick above our heads. I pushed him off, but we were glad when we had got clear of them and safe out of the park. These little events, coming one after the other, left me very jangled in my nerves, and I could see from my companion's petulant manner that his own patience had got to a low ebb.

But our good humour was restored when we saw Lord John Roxton waiting for us upon the platform, his tall, thin figure clad in a yellow tweed shooting-suit. His keen face, with those unforgettable eyes, so fierce and yet so humorous, flushed with pleasure at the sight of us. His ruddy hair was shot with grey, and the furrows upon his brow had been cut a little deeper by Time's chisel, but in all else he was the Lord John who had been our good comrade in the past.

'Hullo, Herr Professor! Hullo, young fellah!' he shouted as he came towards us.

He roared with amusement when he saw the oxygen cylinders upon the porter's trolly behind us.

'So you've got them, too!' he cried. 'Mine is in the van. Whatever can the old dear be after?'

'Have you seen his letter in *The Times*?' I asked.

'What was it?'

'Stuff and nonsense!' said Summerlee, harshly.

'Well, it's at the bottom of this oxygen business, or I am mistaken,' said I.

'Stuff and nonsense!' cried Summerlee again, with quite unnecessary violence.

We had all got into a first-class smoker, and he had already lit the short and charred old briar pipe which seemed to singe the end of his long, aggressive nose.

'Friend Challenger is a clever man,' said he, with great vehemence. 'No one can deny it. It's a fool that denies it. Look at his hat. There's a sixty-ounce brain inside it — a big engine, running smooth, and turning out clean work. Show me the engine-house and I'll tell you the size of the engine. But he is a born charlatan — you've heard me tell him so to his face — a born charlatan, with a kind of dramatic trick of jumping into the limelight. Things are quiet, so friend Challenger sees a chance to set the public talking about him. You don't imagine that he seriously believes all this nonsense about a change in the ether and a danger to the human race? Was ever such a cock-and-bull story in this life?'

He sat like an old white raven, croaking and shaking with sardonic laughter.

A wave of anger passed through me as I listened to Summerlee. It was disgraceful that he should speak thus of the leader who had been the source of all our fame and given us such an experience as no men have ever enjoyed. I had opened my mouth to utter some hot retort, when Lord John got before me.

'You had a scrap once before with old man Challenger,' said he, sternly, 'and you were down and out inside ten seconds. It seems to me, Professor Summerlee, he's beyond your class, and the best you can do with him is to walk wide and leave him alone.'

'Besides,' said I, 'he has been a good friend to every one of us. Whatever his faults may be, he is as straight as a line, and I don't believe he ever speaks evil of his comrades behind their backs.'

'Well said, young fellah-my-lad,' said Lord John Roxton. Then, with a kindly smile, he slapped Professor Summerlee upon his shoulder. 'Come, Herr Professor, we're not going to quarrel at this time of day. We've seen too much together. But keep off the grass when you get near Challenger, for this young fellah and I have a bit of a weakness for the old dear.'

But Summerlee was in no humour for compromise. His face was screwed up in rigid disapproval, and thick curls of angry smoke rolled up from his pipe.

'As to you, Lord John Roxton,' he creaked, 'your opinion upon a matter of science is of as much value in my eyes as my views upon a new type of shotgun would be in yours. I have my own judgment, sir, and I use it in my own way. Because it has misled me once, is that any reason why I should accept without criticism anything, however far-fetched, which this man may care to put forward? Are we to have a Pope of science, with infallible decrees laid down *ex cathedra*, and accepted without question by the poor humble public? I tell you, sir, that I have a brain of my own, and that I should feel myself to be a snob and a slave if I did not use it. If it pleases you to believe this rigmarole about ether and Frauenhofer's lines upon the spectrum, do so by all means, but do not ask one who is older and wiser than yourself to share in your folly. Is it not evident that if the ether were affected to the degree which he maintains, and if it were obnoxious to human health, the result of it would already be apparent upon ourselves?' Here he laughed with uproarious triumph over his own argument. 'Yes, sir, we should already be very far from our normal selves, and instead of sitting quietly discussing scientific problems in a railway train we should be showing actual symptoms of the poison which was working within us. Where do we see any signs of this poisonous cosmic disturbance? Answer me that, sir! Answer me that! Come, come, no evasion! I pin you to an answer!'

I felt more and more angry. There was something very irritating and aggressive in Summerlee's demeanour.

'I think that if you knew more about the facts you might be less positive in your opinion,' said I.

Summerlee took his pipe from his mouth and fixed me with a stony stare.

'Pray what do you mean, sir, by that somewhat impertinent observation?'

'I mean that when I was leaving the office the news editor told me that a telegram had come in confirming the general illness of the Sumatra natives, and adding that the lights had not been lit in the Strait of Sunda.'

'Really, there should be some limits to human folly!' cried Summerlee, in a positive fury. 'Is it possible that you do not realise that ether, if for a moment we adopt Challenger's preposterous supposition, is a universal substance which is the same here as at the other side of the world? Do you for an instant suppose that there is an English ether and a Sumatran ether? Perhaps you imagine that the ether of Kent is in some way superior to the ether of Surrey, through which this train is now bearing us. There really are no bounds to the credulity and ignorance of the average layman. Is it conceivable that the ether in Sumatra should be so deadly as to cause total insensibility at the very time when the ether here has had no appreciable effect upon us whatever? Personally, I can truly say that I never felt stronger in body or better balanced in mind in my life.'

'That may be. I don't profess to be a

scientific man,' said I, 'though I have heard somewhere that the science of one generation is usually the fallacy of the next. But it does not take much common sense to see that as we seem to know so little about ether it might be affected by some local conditions in various parts of the world, and might show an effect over there which would only develop later with us.'

'With 'might' and 'may' you can prove anything,' cried Summerlee furiously. 'Pigs may fly. Yes, sir, pigs *may* fly — but they don't. It is not worth arguing with you. Challenger has filled you with his nonsense and you are both incapable of reason. I had as soon lay arguments before those railway cushions.'

'I must say, Professor Summerlee, that your manners do not seem to have improved since I last had the pleasure of meeting you,' said Lord John, severely.

'You lordlings are not accustomed to hear the truth,' Summerlee answered, with a bitter smile. 'It comes as a bit of a shock, does it not, when someone makes you realise that your title leaves you none the less a very ignorant man?'

'Upon my word, sir,' said Lord John, very stern and rigid, 'if you were a younger man you would not dare to speak to me in so offensive a fashion.'

Summerlee thrust out his chin, with its little wagging tuft of goatee beard.

'I would have you know, sir, that, young or old, there has never been a time in my life when I was afraid to speak my mind to an ignorant coxcomb — yes, sir, an ignorant coxcomb, if you had as many titles as slaves could invent and fools could adopt.'

For a moment Lord John's eyes blazed, and then, with a tremendous effort, he mastered his anger and leaned back in his seat with arms folded and a bitter smile upon his face. To me all this was dreadful and deplorable. Like a wave, the memory of the past swept over me, the good comradeship, the happy, adventurous days — all that we had suffered and worked for and won. That it should have come to this — to insults and abuse! Suddenly I was sobbing — sobbing in loud, gulping, uncontrollable sobs which refused to be concealed. My companions looked at me in surprise. I covered my face with my hands.

'It's all right,' said I. 'Only — only it *is* such a pity!'

'You're ill, young fellah, that's what's amiss with you,' said Lord John. 'I thought you were queer from the first.'

'Your habits, sir, have not mended in these three years,' said Summerlee, shaking his head. 'I also did not fail to observe your strange manner the moment we met. You need not waste your sympathy, Lord John. These tears are purely alcoholic. The man has been drinking. By the way, Lord John, I called you a coxcomb just now, which was perhaps, unduly severe. But the word reminds me of a small accomplishment, trivial but amusing, which I used to possess. You know me as the austere man of science. Can you believe that I once had a well-deserved reputation in several nurseries as a farmyard imitator? Perhaps I can help you to pass the time in a pleasant way. Would it amuse you to hear me crow like a cock?'

'No, sir,' said Lord John, who was still greatly offended; 'it would not amuse me.'

'My imitation of the clucking hen who had just laid an egg was also considered rather above the average. Might I venture?'

'No, sir, no — certainly not.'

But in spite of this earnest prohibition, Professor Summerlee laid down his pipe and for the rest of our journey he entertained — or failed to entertain — us by a succession of bird and animal cries which seemed so absurd that my tears were suddenly changed into boisterous laughter, which must have become quite hysterical as I sat opposite this grave Professor and saw him — or rather heard him — in the character of the uproarious rooster or the puppy whose tail had been trodden upon. Once Lord John passed across his newspaper, upon the margin of which he had written in pencil, 'Poor devil! Mad as a hatter.' No doubt it was very eccentric, and yet the performance struck me as extraordinarily clever and amusing.

While this was going on Lord John leaned forward and told me some interminable story about a buffalo and an Indian rajah, which seemed to me to have neither beginning nor end. Professor Summerlee had just begun to chirrup like a canary, and Lord John to get to the climax of his story, when the train drew up at Jarvis Brook, which had been given us as the station for Rotherfield.

And there was Challenger to meet us. His appearance was glorious. Not all the turkey-cocks in creation could match the slow, high-stepping dignity with which he paraded his own railway station, and the benignant smile of condescending encouragement with which he regarded everybody around him. If he had changed in anything since the days of old, it was that his points had become accentuated. The huge head and broad sweep of forehead, with its plastered lock of black hair, seemed even greater than before. His black beard poured forward in a more impressive cascade, and his clear grey eyes, with their insolent and sardonic eyelids, were even more masterful than of yore.

He gave me the amused handshake and encouraging smile which the headmaster bestows upon the small boy, and, having greeted the others and helped to collect their bags and their cylinders of oxygen, he stowed us and them away in a large motorcar which was driven by the same impassive Austin, the man of few words, whom I had seen in the character of butler upon the occasion of my first eventful visit to the Professor. Our journey led us up a winding hill through beautiful country. I sat in front with the chauffeur, but behind me my three comrades seemed to me to be all talking together. Lord John was still struggling with his buffalo story, so far as I could make out, while once again I heard, as of old, the deep rumble of Challenger and the insistent accents of Summerlee, as their brains locked in high and fierce scientific debate. Suddenly Austin slanted his mahogany face towards me without taking his eyes from his steering-wheel.

'I'm under notice,' said he.

'Dear me!' said I.

Everything seemed strange today. Everyone

said queer, unexpected things. It was like a dream.

'It's forty-seven times,' said Austin, reflectively.

'When do you go?' I asked, for want of some better observation.

'I don't go,' said Austin.

The conversation seemed to have ended there, but presently he came back to it.

'If I was to go, who would look after 'im?' He jerked his head towards his master. 'Who would 'e get to serve 'im?'

'Someone else,' I suggested lamely.

'Not 'e. No one would stay a week. If I was to go, that 'ouse would run down like a watch with the mainspring out. I'm telling you because you're 'is friend, and you ought to know. If I was to take 'im at 'is word — but there, I wouldn't have the 'eart. 'e and the missus would be like two babes left out in a bundle. I'm just everything. And then 'e goes and gives me notice.'

'Why would no one stay?' I asked.

'Well, they wouldn't make allowances, same as I do. 'e's a very clever man, the master — so clever that 'e's clean balmy sometimes. I've seen 'im right off 'is onion, and no error. Well, look what 'e did this morning.'

'What did he do?'

26

Austin bent over to me.

''e bit the 'ousekeeper,' said he, in a hoarse whisper.

'Bit her?'

'Yes, sir. Bit 'er on the leg. I saw 'er with my own eyes startin' a Marathon from the 'all-door.'

'Good gracious!'

'So you'd say, sir, if you could see some of the goings-on. 'e don't make friends with the neighbours. There's some of them thinks that when 'e was up among those monsters you wrote about, it was just ''ome, Sweet 'ome,' for the master, and 'e was never in fitter company. That's what they say. But I've served 'im ten years, and I'm fond of 'im, and, mind you, 'e's a great man, when all's said an' done, and it's an honour to serve 'im. But 'e does try one cruel at times. Now look at that, sir. That ainwhat you might call old-fashioned 'ospitality, is it now? Just you read it for yourself.'

The car on its lowest speed had ground its way up a steep, curving ascent. At the corner a noticeboard peered over a well-clipped hedge. As Austin said, it was not difficult to read, for the words were few and arresting: 'Warning. Visitors, Pressmen, and Mendicants are not encouraged. G. E. Challenger.'

'No, it's not what you might call 'earty,'

said Austin, shaking his head and glancing up at the deplorable placard. 'It wouldn't look well in a Christmas-card. I beg your pardon, sir, for I haven't spoke as much as this for many a long year, but today my feelings seem to 'ave got the better of me. 'e can sack me till 'e's blue in the face, but I ain't going, and that's flat. I'm 'is man and 'e's my master, and so it will be, I expect, to the end of the chapter.'

We had passed between the white posts of a gate and up a curving drive, lined with rhododendron bushes. Beyond stood a low brick house, picked out with white woodwork, very comfortable and pretty. Mrs Challenger, a small, dainty, smiling figure, stood in the open doorway to welcome us.

'Well, my dear,' said Challenger, bustling out of the car, 'here are our visitors. It is something new for us to have visitors, is it not? No love lost between us and our neighbours, is there? If they could get rat poison into our baker's cart, I expect it would be there.'

'It's dreadful — dreadful!' cried the lady, between laughter and tears. 'George is always quarrelling with everyone. We haven't a friend on the countryside.'

'It enables me to concentrate my attention upon my incomparable wife,' said Challenger,

28

passing his short, thick arm round her waist. Picture a gorilla and a gazelle, and you have the pair of them. 'Come, come, these gentlemen are tired from the journey, and luncheon should be ready. Has Sarah returned?'

The lady shook her head ruefully, and the Professor laughed loudly and stroked his beard in his masterful fashion.

'Austin,' he cried, 'when you have put up the car you will kindly help your mistress to lay the lunch. Now, gentlemen, will you please step into my study, for there are one or two very urgent things which I am anxious to say to you.'

# 2

## The Tide of Death

As we crossed the hall the telephone-bell
rang, and we were the involuntary auditors of
Professor Challenger's end of the ensuing
dialogue. I say 'we,' but no one within a
hundred yards could have failed to hear the
booming of that monstrous voice, which
reverberated through the house. His answers
lingered in my mind.

'Yes, yes, of course, it is I . . . Yes, certainly,
the Professor Challenger, the famous Professor, who else? . . . Of course, every word of it,
otherwise I should not have written it . . . I
shouldn't be surprised . . . There is every
indication of it . . . Within a day or so at the
furthest . . . Well, I can't help that, can I?
. . . Very unpleasant, no doubt, but I rather
fancy it will affect more important people
than you. There is no use whining about it
. . . No, I couldn't possibly. You must take
your chance . . . That's enough, sir. Nonsense! I have something more important to
do than to listen to such twaddle.'

He shut off with a crash and led us upstairs

into a large, airy apartment which formed his study. On the great mahogany desk seven or eight unopened telegrams were lying.

'Really,' he said, as he gathered them up, 'I begin to think that it would save my correspondents' money if I were to adopt a telegraphic address. Possibly 'Noah, Rotherfield,' would be the most appropriate.'

As usual when he made an obscure joke, he leaned against the desk and bellowed in a paroxysm of laughter, his hands shaking so that he could hardly open the envelopes.

'Noah! Noah!' he gasped, with a face of beetroot, while Lord John and I smiled in sympathy, and Summerlee, like a dyspeptic goat, wagged his head in sardonic disagreement. Finally Challenger, still rumbling and exploding, began to open his telegrams. The three of us stood in the bow window and occupied ourselves in admiring the magnificent view.

It was certainly worth looking at. The road in its gentle curves had really brought us to a considerable elevation — seven hundred feet, as we afterwards discovered. Challenger's house was on the very edge of the hill, and from its southern face, in which was the study window, one looked across the vast stretch of the Weald to where the gentle curves of the South Downs formed an undulating horizon.

31

In a cleft of the hills a haze of smoke marked the position of Lewes. Immediately at our feet there lay a rolling plain of heather, with the long, vivid green stretches of the Crowborough golf course, all dotted with the players. A little to the south, through an opening in the woods, we could see a section of the main line from London to Brighton. In the immediate foreground, under our very noses, was a small enclosed yard, in which stood the car which had brought us from the station.

An ejaculation from Challenger caused us to turn. He had read his telegrams and had arranged them in a little methodical pile upon his desk. His broad, rugged face, or as much of it as was visible over the matted beard, was still deeply flushed, and he seemed to be under the influence of some strong excitement.

'Well, gentlemen,' he said, in a voice as if he was addressing a public meeting, 'this is indeed an interesting reunion, and it takes place under extraordinary — I may say unprecedented — circumstances. May I ask if you have observed anything upon your journey from town?'

'The only thing which I observed,' said Summerlee, with a sour smile, 'was that our young friend here has not improved in his manners during the years that have passed. I am sorry to state that I have had to seriously complain of his conduct in the train, and I should be wanting in frankness if I did not say that it has left a most unpleasant impression in my mind.'

'Well, well, we all get a bit prosy sometimes,' said Lord John. 'The young fellah meant no real harm. After all, he's an International, so if he takes half an hour to describe a game of football he has more right to do it than most folk.'

'Half an hour to describe a game!' I cried, indignantly. 'Why, it was you that took half an hour with some long-winded story about a buffalo. Professor Summerlee will be my witness.'

'I can hardly judge which of you was the most utterly wearisome,' said Summerlee. 'I declare to you, Challenger, that I never wish to hear of football or of buffaloes so long as I live.'

'I have never said one word today about football,' I protested.

Lord John gave a shrill whistle, and Summerlee shook his head sadly.

'So early in the day, too,' said he. 'It is indeed deplorable. As I sat there in sad but thoughtful silence — '

'In silence!' cried Lord John. 'Why, you were doin' a music-hall turn of imitations all the way — more like a runaway gramophone than a man.'

Summerlee drew himself up in bitter protest. 'You are pleased to be facetious, Lord John,' said he, with a face of vinegar.

'Why, dash it all, this is clear madness,' cried Lord John. 'Each of us seems to know what the others did and none of us knows what he did himself. Let's put it all together from the first. We got into a first-class smoker, that's clear, ain't it? Then we began to quarrel over friend Challenger's letter in *The Times*.'

'Oh, you did, did you?' rumbled our host, his eyelids beginning to droop.

'You said, Summerlee, that there was no possible truth in his contention.'

'Dear me!' said Challenger, puffing out his chest and stroking his beard. 'No possible truth! I seem to have heard the words before. And may I ask with what arguments the great and famous Professor Summerlee proceeded to demolish the humble individual who had ventured to express an opinion upon a matter of scientific possibility? Perhaps before he exterminates that unfortunate nonentity he will condescend to give some reasons for the adverse views which he has formed.'

He bowed and shrugged and spread open his hands as he spoke with his elaborate and elephantine sarcasm.

'The reason was simple enough,' said the dogged Summerlee. 'I contended that, if the ether surrounding the earth was so toxic in one quarter that it produced dangerous symptoms, it was hardly likely that we three in the railway carriage should be entirely unaffected.'

The explanation only brought uproarious merriment from Challenger. He laughed until everything in the room seemed to rattle and quiver.

'Our worthy Summerlee is, not for the first time, somewhat out of touch with the facts of the situation,' said he at last, mopping his heated brow. 'Now, gentlemen, I cannot make my point better than by detailing to you what I have myself done this morning. You will the more easily condone any mental aberration upon your own part when you realise that even I have had moments when my balance has been disturbed. We have had for some years in this household a housekeeper — one Sarah, with whose second name I have never attempted to burden my memory. She is a woman of a severe and forbidding aspect, prim and demure in her bearing, very impassive in her nature, and never known within our experience to show signs of any emotion. As I sat alone at my breakfast — Mrs Challenger is in the habit of keeping to her room of a morning — it suddenly entered my head that it would be entertaining and instructive to see whether I could find any limits to this woman's imperturbability. I devised a simple but effective experiment. Having upset a small vase of flowers which stood in the centre of the cloth, I rang the bell and slipped under the table. She entered, and, seeing the room empty, imagined that I had withdrawn to the study. As I had expected, she approached and leaned over the table to replace the vase. I had a vision of a cotton stocking and an elastic-sided boot. Protruding my head, I sank my teeth into the calf of her leg. The experiment was successful beyond belief. For some moments she stood paralysed, staring down at my head. Then with a shriek she tore herself free and rushed from the room. I pursued her with some thoughts of an explanation, but she flew down the drive, and some minutes afterwards I was able to pick her out with my field-glasses travelling very rapidly in a south-westerly direction. I tell you the anecdote for what it is worth. I drop it into your brains and await its germination. Is it illuminative? Has it conveyed anything to your minds? What do you think of it, Lord John?'

Lord John shook his head gravely.

'You'll be gettin' into serious trouble some of these days if you don't put a brake on,' said he.

'Perhaps you have some observation to make, Summerlee?'

'You should drop all work instantly, Challenger, and take three months in a German watering-place,' said he.

'Profound! profound!' cried Challenger. 'Now, my young friend, is it possible that wisdom may come from you where your seniors have so signally failed?'

And it did. I say it with all modesty, but it did. Of course, it all seems obvious enough to you who know what occurred, but it was not so very clear when everything was new. But it came on me suddenly with the full force of absolute conviction.

'Poison!' I cried.

Then, even as I said the word, my mind flashed back over the whole morning's experiences, past Lord John with his buffalo, past my own hysterical tears, past the outrageous conduct of Professor Summerlee, to the queer happenings in London, the row in the park, the driving of the chauffeur, the quarrel at the oxygen warehouse. Everything fitted suddenly into its place.

'Of course,' I cried again. 'It is poison. We are all poisoned.'

'Exactly,' said Challenger, rubbing his hands; 'we are all poisoned. Our planet has swum into the poison belt of ether, and is now flying deeper into it at the rate of some millions of miles a minute. Our young friend has expressed the cause of all our troubles and perplexities in a single word, 'Poison.' '

We looked at each other in amazed silence. No comment seemed to meet the situation.

'There is a mental inhibition by which such symptoms can be checked and controlled,' said Challenger. 'I cannot expect to find it developed in all of you to the same point which it has reached in me, for I suppose that the strength of our different mental processes bears some proportion to each other. But no doubt it is appreciable even in our young friend here. After the little outburst of high spirits which so alarmed my domestic I sat down and reasoned with myself. I put it to myself that I had never before felt impelled to bite any of my household. The impulse had then been an abnormal one. In an instant I perceived the truth. My pulse upon examination was ten beats above the usual, and my reflexes were increased. I called upon my higher and saner self, the real G.E.C., seated serene and impregnable behind all mere molecular disturbance. I summoned him, I say, to watch the foolish and mental tricks which the poison would play. I found that I was indeed the master. I could recognise and control a disordered mind. It was a remarkable exhibition of the victory of mind over matter, for it was a victory over that particular form of matter which is most intimately connected with mind. I might almost say that mind was at fault, and that personality controlled it. Thus, when my wife came downstairs and I was impelled to slip behind the door and alarm her by some wild cry as she entered, I was able to stifle the impulse and to greet her with dignity and restraint. An overpowering desire to quack like a duck was met and mastered in the same fashion. Later, when I descended to order the car and found Austin bending over it absorbed in repairs, I controlled my open hand even after I had lifted it, and refrained from giving him an experience which would possibly have caused him to follow in the steps of the housekeeper. On the contrary, I touched him on the shoulder and ordered the car to be at the door in time to meet your train. At the present instant I am most forcibly tempted to take Professor Summerlee by that silly old beard of his, and to shake his head violently backwards and forwards. And yet, as you see, I am perfectly restrained. Let me commend my example to you.'

'I'll look out for that buffalo,' said Lord John.

'And I for the football match.'

'It may be that you are right, Challenger,' said Summerlee, in a chastened voice. 'I am willing to admit that my turn of mind is critical rather than constructive, and that I am not a ready convert to any new theory, especially when it happens to be so unusual and fantastic as this one. However, as I cast my mind back over the events of the morning, and as I reconsider the fatuous conduct of my companions, I find it easy to believe that some poison of an exciting kind was responsible for their symptoms.'

Challenger slapped his colleague good-humouredly upon the shoulder. 'We progress,' said he. 'Decidedly we progress.'

'And pray, sir,' asked Summerlee, humbly, 'what is your opinion as to the present outlook?'

'With your permission I will say a few words upon that subject.' He seated himself upon his desk, his short, stumpy legs swinging in front of him. 'We are assisting at a tremendous and awful function. It is, in my opinion, the end of the world.'

The end of the world! Our eyes turned to the great bow-window and we looked out at the summer beauty of the countryside, the

40

long slopes of heather, the great country houses, the cosy farms, the pleasure-seekers upon the links. The end of the world! One had often heard the words, but the idea that they could ever have an immediate practical significance, that it should not be at some vague date, but now, today, that was a tremendous, a staggering thought. We were all struck solemn and waited in silence for Challenger to continue. His overpowering presence and appearance lent such force to the solemnity of his words that for a moment all the crudities and absurdities of the man vanished, and he loomed before us as something majestic and beyond the range of ordinary humanity. Then to me, at least, there came back the cheering recollection of how twice since we had entered the room he had roared with laughter. Surely, I thought, there are limits to mental detachment. The crisis cannot be so great or so pressing, after all.

'You will conceive a bunch of grapes,' said he, 'which are covered by some infinitesimal but noxious bacillus. The gardener passes it through a disinfecting medium. It may be that he desires his grapes to be cleaner. It may be that he needs space to breed some fresh bacillus less noxious than the last. He dips it into the poison and they are gone. Our Gardener is, in my opinion, about to dip the solar system, and the human bacillus, the little mortal vibrio which twisted and wriggled upon the outer rind of the earth, will in an instant be sterilised out of existence.'

Again there was silence. It was broken by the high trill of the telephone-bell.

'There is one of our bacilli squeaking for help,' said he, with a grim smile. 'They are beginning to realise that their continued existence is not really one of the necessities of the Universe.'

He was gone from the room for a minute or two. I remember that none of us spoke in his absence. The situation seemed beyond all words or comments.

'The medical officer of health for Brighton,' said he, when he returned. 'The symptoms are for some reason developing more rapidly upon the sea-level. Our seven hundred feet of elevation give us an advantage. Folk seem to have learned that I am the first authority upon the question. No doubt it comes from my letter in *The Times*. That was the mayor of a provincial town with whom I talked when we first arrived. You may have heard me upon the telephone. He seemed to put an entirely inflated value upon his own life. I helped him to readjust his ideas.'

Summerlee had risen and was standing by

the window. His thin, bony hands were trembling with his emotion.

'Challenger,' said he, earnestly, 'this thing is too serious for mere futile argument. Do not suppose that I desire to irritate you by any question I may ask. But I put it to you whether there may not be some fallacy in your information or in your reasoning. There is the sun shining as brightly as ever in the blue sky. There are the heather and the flowers and the birds. There are the folk enjoying themselves upon the golf-links, and the labourers yonder cutting the corn. You tell us that they and we may be upon the very brink of destruction — that this sunlit day may be that day of doom which the human race has so long awaited. So far as we know, you found this tremendous judgment upon what? Upon some abnormal lines in a spectrum — upon rumours from Sumatra — upon some curious personal excitement which we have discerned in each other. This latter symptom is not so marked but that you and we could, by a deliberate effort, control it. You need not stand on ceremony with us, Challenger. We have all faced death together before now. Speak out, and let us know exactly where we stand, and what, in your opinion, are our prospects for our future.'

It was a brave, good speech, a speech from

that staunch and strong spirit which lay behind all the acidities and angularities of the old zoologist. Lord John rose and shook him by the hand.

'My sentiment to a tick,' said he. 'Now, Challenger, it's up to you to tell us where we are. We ain't nervous folk, as you know well; but when it comes to makin' a weekend visit and finding you've run full butt into the Day of Judgment, it wants a bit of explainin'. What's the danger, and how much of it is there, and what are we goin' to do to meet it?'

He stood, tall and strong, in the sunshine at the window, with his brown hand upon the shoulder of Summerlee. I was lying back in an armchair, an extinguished cigarette between my lips, in that sort of half-dazed state in which impressions become exceedingly distinct. It may have been a new phase of the poisoning, but the delirious promptings had all passed away, and were succeeded by an exceedingly languid and, at the same time, perceptive state of mind. I was a spectator. It did not seem to be any personal concern of mine. But here were three strong men at a great crisis, and it was fascinating to observe them. Challenger bent his heavy brows and stroked his beard before he answered. One could see that he was very carefully weighing his words.

'What was the last news when you left London?' he asked.

'I was at the *Gazette* office about ten,' said I. 'There was a Reuter just come in from Singapore to the effect that the sickness seemed to be universal in Sumatra, and that the lighthouses had not been lit in consequence.'

'Events have been moving somewhat rapidly since then,' said Challenger, picking up his pile of telegrams. 'I am in close touch both with the authorities and with the Press, so that news is converging upon me from all parts. There is, in fact, a general and very insistent demand that I should come to London; but I see no good end to be served. From the accounts the poisonous effect begins with mental excitement; the rioting in Paris this morning is said to have been very violent, and the Welsh colliers are in a state of uproar. So far as the evidence to hand can be trusted, this stimulative stage, which varies much in races and in individuals, is succeeded by a certain exaltation and mental lucidity — I seem to discern some signs of it in our young friend here — which, after an appreciable interval, turns to coma, deepening rapidly into death. I fancy, so far as my toxicology carries me, that there are some vegetable nerve poisons — '

'Datura,' suggested Summerlee.

'Excellent!' cried Challenger. 'It would make for scientific precision if we named our toxic agent. Let it be daturon. To you, my dear Summerlee, belongs the honour — posthumous, alas! but none the less unique — of having given a name to the universal destroyer, the great Gardener's disinfectant. The symptoms of daturon, then, may be taken to be such as I indicate. That it will involve the whole world and that no life can possibly remain behind seems to me to be certain, since ether is a universal medium. Up to now it has been capricious in the places which it has attacked, but the difference is only a matter of a few hours, and it is like an advancing tide which covers one strip of sand and then another, running hither and thither in irregular streams, until at last it has submerged it all. There are laws at work in connection with the action and distribution of daturon which would have been of deep interest had the time at our disposal permitted us to study them. So far as I can trace them' — here he glanced over his telegrams — 'the less developed races have been the first to respond to its influence. There are deplorable accounts from Africa, and the Australian aborigines appear to have been already exterminated. The Northern

46

races have as yet shown greater resisting power than the Southern. This, you see, is dated from Marseilles at nine-forty-five this morning. I give it to you verbatim: 'All night delirious excitement throughout Provence. Tumult of vine growers at Nîmes. Socialistic upheaval at Toulon. Sudden illness attended by coma attacked population this morning. *Peste foudroyant*. Great numbers of dead in the streets. Paralysis of business and universal chaos.'

'An hour later came the following, from the same source: 'We are threatened with utter extermination. Cathedrals and churches full to overflowing. The dead outnumber the living. It is inconceivable and horrible. Decease seems to be painless, but swift and inevitable.'

'There is a similar telegram from Paris, where the development is not yet as acute. India and Persia appear to be utterly wiped out. The Slavonic population of Austria is down, while the Teutonic has hardly been affected. Speaking generally, the dwellers upon the plains and upon the seashore seem, so far as my limited information goes, to have felt the effects more rapidly than those inland or on the heights. Even a little elevation makes a considerable difference, and perhaps if there be a survivor of the human race, he will again be found upon the summit of some Ararat. Even our own little hill may presently prove to be a temporary island amid a sea of disaster. But at the present rate of advance a few short hours will submerge us all.'

Lord John Roxton wiped his brow.

'What beats me,' said he, 'is how you could sit there laughin' with that stack of telegrams under your hand. I've seen death as often as most folk; but universal death — it's awful!'

'As to the laughter,' said Challenger, 'you will bear in mind that, like yourselves, I have not been exempt from the stimulating cerebral effects of the etheric poison. But as to the horror with which universal death appears to inspire you, I would put it to you that it is somewhat exaggerated. If you were sent to sea alone in an open boat to some unknown destination, your heart might well sink within you. The isolation, the uncertainty, would oppress you. But if your voyage were made in a goodly ship, which bore within it all your relations and your friends, you would feel that, however uncertain your destination might still remain, you would at least have one common and simultaneous experience which would hold you to the end in the same close communion. A lonely death may be terrible, but a universal one, as painless as this would appear to be, is not, in my judgment, a matter for apprehension. Indeed, I could sympathise with the person who took the view that the horror lay in the idea of surviving when all that is learned, famous, and exalted had passed away.'

'What, then, do you propose to do?' asked Summerlee, who had for once nodded his assent to the reasoning of his brother scientist.

'To take our lunch,' said Challenger, as the boom of a gong sounded through the house. 'We have a cook whose omelettes are only excelled by her cutlets. We can but trust that no cosmic disturbance has dulled her excellent abilities. My Scharzberger of '96 must also be rescued, so far as our earnest and united efforts can do it, from what would be a deplorable waste of a great vintage.' He levered his great bulk off the desk, upon which he had sat while he announced the doom of the planet. 'Come,' said he. 'If there is little time left, there is the more need that we should spend it in sober and reasonable enjoyment.'

And, indeed, it proved to be a very merry meal. It is true that we could not forget our awful situation. The full solemnity of the event loomed ever at the back of our minds and tempered our thoughts. But surely it is the soul which has never faced Death which shies strongly from it at the end. To each of us men it had, for one great epoch in our lives, been a familiar presence. As to the lady, she leaned upon the strong guidance of her mighty husband and was well content to go whither his path might lead. The future was our Fate. The present was our own. We passed it in goodly comradeship and gentle merriment. Our minds were, as I have said, singularly lucid. Even I struck sparks at times. As to Challenger, he was wonderful! Never have I so realised the elemental greatness of the man, the sweep and power of his understanding. Summerlee drew him on with his chorus of sub-acid criticism, while Lord John and I laughed at the contest; and the lady, her hand upon his sleeve, controlled the bellowings of the philosopher. Life, death, fate, the destiny of man — these were the stupendous subjects of that memorable hour, made vital by the fact that as the meal progressed strange, sudden exaltations in my mind and tinglings in my limbs proclaimed that the invisible tide of Death was slowly and gently rising around us. Once I saw Lord John put his hand suddenly to his eyes, and once Summerlee dropped back for an instant in his chair. Each breath we breathed was charged with strange forces. And yet our minds were happy and at ease. Presently

Austin laid the cigarettes upon the table and was about to withdraw.

'Austin!' said his master.

'Yes, sir?'

'I thank you for your faithful service.'

A smile stole over the servant's gnarled face.

'I've done my duty, sir.'

'I'm expecting the end of the world today, Austin.'

'Yes, sir. What time, sir?'

'I can't say, Austin. Before evening.'

'Very good, sir.'

The taciturn Austin saluted and withdrew. Challenger lit a cigarette, and, drawing his chair to his wife's, he took her hand in his.

'You know how matters stand, dear,' said he. 'I have explained it also to our friends here. You're not afraid, are you?'

'It won't be painful, George?'

'No more than laughing-gas at the dentist's. Every time you have had it you have practically died.'

'But that is a pleasant sensation.'

'So may death be. The worn-out bodily machine can't record its impression, but we know the mental pleasure which lies in a dream or a trance. Nature may build a beautiful door and hang it with many a gauzy and shimmering curtain to make an entrance to the new life for our wondering souls. In all my probings of the actual, I have always found wisdom and kindness at the core; and if ever the frightened mortal needs tenderness, it is surely as he makes the passage perilous from life to life. No, Summerlee, I will have none of your materialism, for I, at least, am too great a thing to end in mere physical constituents, a packet of salts and three bucketfuls of water. Here — here' — and he beat his great head with his huge, hairy fist — 'there is something which uses matter, but is not of it — something which might destroy death, but which Death can never destroy.'

'Talkin' of death,' said Lord John. 'I'm a Christian of sorts, but it seems to me there was somethin' mighty natural in those ancestors of ours who were buried with their axes and bows and arrows and the like, same as if they were livin' on just the same as they used to. I don't know,' he added, looking round the table in a shamefaced way, 'that I wouldn't feel more homely myself if I was put away with my old .450 Express and the fowlin'-piece, the shorter one with the rubbered stock, and a clip or two of cartridges — just a fool's fancy, of course, but there it is. How does it strike you, Herr Professor?'

'Well,' said Summerlee, 'since you ask my opinion, it strikes me as an indefensible throwback to the Stone Age or before it. I'm of the twentieth century myself, and would wish to die like a reasonable civilised man. I don't know that I am more afraid of death than the rest of you, for I am an oldish man, and, come what may, I can't have very much longer to live; but it is all against my nature to sit waiting without a struggle like a sheep for the butcher. Is it quite certain, Challenger, that there is nothing we can do?'

'To save us — nothing,' said Challenger. 'To prolong our lives a few hours, and thus to see the evolution of this mighty tragedy before we are actually involved in it — that may prove to be within my powers. I have taken certain steps — '

'The oxygen?'

'Exactly. The oxygen.'

'But what can oxygen effect in the face of a poisoning of the ether? There is not a greater difference in quality between a brickbat and a gas than there is between oxygen and ether. They are different planes of matter. They cannot impinge upon one another. Come, Challenger, you could not defend such a proposition.'

'My good Summerlee, this etheric poison is most certainly influenced by material agents.

We see it in the methods and distribution of the outbreak. We should not a priori have expected it, but it is undoubtedly a fact. Hence I am strongly of opinion that a gas like oxygen, which increases the vitality and the resisting power of the body, would be extremely likely to delay the action of what you have so happily named the daturon. It may be that I am mistaken, but I have every confidence in the correctness of my reasoning.'

'Well,' said Lord John, 'if we've got to sit suckin' at those tubes like so many babies with their bottles, I'm not takin' any.'

'There will be no need for that,' Challenger answered. 'We have made arrangements — it is to my wife that you chiefly owe it — that her boudoir shall be made as airtight as is practicable. With matting and varnished paper.'

'Good heavens, Challenger, you don't suppose you can keep out ether with varnished paper?'

'Really, my friend, you are a trifle perverse in missing the point. It is not to keep out the ether that we have gone to such trouble. It is to keep in the oxygen. I trust that if we can ensure an atmosphere hyper-oxygenated to a certain point, we may be able to retain our senses. I had two tubes of the gas and you have brought me three more. It is not much, but it is something.'

'How long will they last?'

'I have not an idea. We will not turn them on until our symptoms become unbearable. Then we shall dole the gas out as it is urgently needed. It may give us some hours, possibly even some days, on which we may look out upon a blasted world. Our own fate is delayed to that extent, and we will have the very singular experience, we five, of being, in all probability, the absolute rearguard of the human race upon its march into the unknown. Perhaps you will be kind enough now to give me a hand with the cylinders. It seems to me that the atmosphere already grows somewhat more oppressive.'

# 3

## Submerged

The chamber which was destined to be the scene of our unforgettable experience was a charmingly feminine sitting-room, some fourteen or sixteen feet square. At the end of it, divided by a curtain of red velvet, was a small apartment which formed the Professor's dressing-room. This in turn opened into a large bedroom. The curtain was still hanging, but the boudoir and dressing-room could be taken as one chamber for the purposes of our experiment. One door and the window-frame had been plastered round with varnished paper, so as to be practically sealed. Above the other door, which opened on to the landing, there hung a fanlight which could be drawn by a cord when some ventilation became absolutely necessary. A large shrub in a tub stood in each corner.

'How to get rid of our excessive carbon dioxide without unduly wasting our oxygen is a delicate and vital question,' said Challenger, looking round him after the five iron tubes had been laid side by side against the wall.

'With longer time for preparation I could have brought the whole concentrated force of my intelligence to bear more fully upon the problem, but as it is we must do what we can. The shrubs will be of some small service. Two of the oxygen tubes are ready to be turned on at an instant's notice, so that we cannot be taken unawares. At the same time, it would be well not to go far from the room, as the crisis may be a sudden and urgent one.'

There was a broad, low window opening out upon a balcony. The view beyond was the same as that which we had already admired from the study. Looking out, I could see no sign of disorder anywhere. There was a road curving down the side of the hill, under my very eyes. A cab from the station, one of those prehistoric survivals which are only to be found in our country villages, was toiling slowly up the hill. Lower down was a nurse-girl wheeling a perambulator and leading a second child by the hand. The blue reeks of smoke from the cottages gave the whole widespread landscape an air of settled order and homely comfort. Nowhere in the blue heaven or on the sunlit earth was there any foreshadowing of a catastrophe. The harvesters were back in the fields once more and the golfers, in pairs and fours, were still streaming round the links. There was so strange a turmoil within my own head, and such a jangling of my over-strung nerves, that the indifference of these people was amazing.

'Those fellows don't seem to feel any ill effects,' said I, pointing down at the links.

'Have you played golf?' asked Lord John.

'No, I have not.'

'Well, young fellah, when you do you'll learn that once fairly out on a round, it would take the crack of doom to stop a true golfer. Halloa! There's that telephone-bell again.'

From time to time during and after lunch the high, insistent ring had summoned the Professor. He gave us the news as it came through to him in a few curt sentences. Such terrific items had never been registered in the world's history before. The great shadow was creeping up from the South like a rising tide of death. Egypt had gone through its delirium and was now comatose. Spain and Portugal, after a wild frenzy in which the Clericals and the Anarchists had fought most desperately, were now fallen silent. No cable messages were received any longer from South America. In North America the Southern States, after some terrible racial rioting, had succumbed to the poison. North of Maryland the effect was not yet marked, and in Canada it was hardly perceptible. Belgium, Holland, and Denmark had each in turn been affected.

Despairing messages were flashing from every quarter to the great centres of learning, to the chemists and the doctors of worldwide repute, imploring their advice. The astronomers, too, were deluged with enquiries. Nothing could be done. The thing was universal and beyond our human knowledge or control. It was death — painless but inevitable — death for young and old, for weak and strong, for rich and poor, without hope or possibility of escape. Such was the news which, in scattered distracted messages, the telephone had brought us. The great cities already knew their fate, and so far as we could gather were preparing to meet it with dignity and resignation. Yet here were our golfers and labourers like the lambs who gambol under the shadow of the knife. It seemed amazing. And yet how could they know? It had all come upon us in one giant stride. What was there in the morning paper to alarm them? And now it was but three in the afternoon. Even as we looked some rumour seemed to have spread, for we saw the reapers hurrying from the fields. Some of the golfers were returning to the clubhouse. They were running as if taking refuge from a shower. Their little caddies trailed behind them. Others were continuing their game. The nurse had turned and was pushing her perambulator hurriedly up the hill again. I noticed that she had her hand to her brow. The cab had stopped and the tired horse, with his head sunk to his knees, was resting. Above there was a perfect summer sky — one huge vault of unbroken blue, save for a few fleecy white clouds over the distant downs. If the human race must die today, it was at least upon a glorious deathbed. And yet all that gentle loveliness of Nature made this terrific and wholesale destruction the more pitiable and awful. Surely it was too goodly a residence that we should be so swiftly, so ruthlessly, evicted from it!

But I have said that the telephone-bell had rung once more. Suddenly I heard Challenger's tremendous voice from the hall.

'Malone!' he cried. 'You are wanted.'

I rushed down to the instrument. It was McArdle speaking from London.

'That you, Mr Malone?' cried his familiar voice. 'Mr Malone, there are terrible goings-on in London. For God's sake, see if Professor Challenger can suggest anything that can be done.'

'He can suggest nothing, sir,' I answered. 'He regards the crisis as universal and inevitable. We have some oxygen here, but it can only defer our fate for a few hours.'

'Oxygen!' cried the agonised voice. 'There

is no time to get any. The office has been a perfect pandemonium ever since you left in the morning. Now half of the staff are insensible. I am weighed down with heaviness myself. From my window I can see the people lying thick in Fleet Street. The traffic is all held up. Judging by the last telegrams, the whole world — '

His voice had been sinking, and suddenly stopped. An instant later I heard through the telephone a muffled thud, as if his head had fallen forward on the desk.

'Mr McArdle!' I cried. 'Mr McArdle!'

There was no answer. I knew as I replaced the receiver that I should never hear his voice again.

At that instant, just as I took a step backwards from the telephone, the thing was on us. It was as if we were bathers, up to our shoulders in water, who suddenly are submerged by a rolling wave. An invisible hand seemed to have quietly closed round my throat and to be gently pressing the life from me. I was conscious of immense oppression upon my chest, great tightness within my head, a loud singing in my ears, and bright flashes before my eyes. I staggered to the balustrades of the stair. At the same moment, rushing and snorting like a wounded buffalo, Challenger dashed past me, a terrible vision, with red-purple face, engorged eyes, and bristling hair. His little wife, insensible to all appearance, was slung over his great shoulder, and he blundered and thundered up the stair, scrambling and tripping, but carrying himself and her through sheer will-force through that mephitic atmosphere to the haven of temporary safety. At the sight of his effort I too rushed up the steps, clambering, falling, clutching at the rail, until I tumbled half senseless upon my face on the upper landing. Lord John's fingers of steel were in the collar of my coat, and a moment later I was stretched upon my back, unable to speak or move, on the boudoir carpet. The woman lay beside me and Summerlee was bunched in a chair by the window, his head nearly touching his knees. As in a dream I saw Challenger, like a monstrous beetle, crawling slowly across the floor, and a moment later I heard the gentle hissing of the escaping oxygen. Challenger breathed two or three times with enormous gulps, his lungs roaring as he drew in the vital gas.

'It works!' he cried exultantly. 'My reasoning has been justified!' He was up on his feet again, alert and strong. With a tube in his hand he rushed over to his wife and held it to her face. In a few seconds she moaned, stirred, and sat up. He turned to me, and I felt the tide of life stealing warmly through my arteries. My reason told me that it was but a little respite, and yet, carelessly as we talk of its value, every hour of existence now seemed an inestimable thing. Never have I known such a thrill of sensuous joy as came with that freshet of life. The weight fell away from my lungs, the band loosened from my brow, a sweet feeling of peace and gentle, languid comfort stole over me. I lay watching Summerlee revive under the same remedy, and finally Lord John took his turn. He sprang to his feet and gave me a hand to rise, while Challenger picked up his wife and laid her on the settee.

'Oh, George, I am so sorry you brought me back,' she said, holding him by the hand. 'The door of death is indeed, as you said, hung with beautiful, shimmering curtains; for, once the choking feeling had passed, it was all unspeakably soothing and beautiful. Why have you dragged me back?'

'Because I wish that we make the passage together. We have been together so many years. It would be sad to fall apart at the supreme moment.'

For a moment in his tender voice I caught a glimpse of a new Challenger, something very far from the bullying, ranting, arrogant man who had alternately amazed and offended his generation. Here in the shadow of death was the innermost Challenger, the man who had won and held a woman's love. Suddenly his mood changed and he was our strong captain once again.

'Alone of all mankind I saw and foretold this catastrophe,' said he, with a ring of exultation and scientific triumph in his voice. 'As to you, my good Summerlee, I trust your last doubts have been resolved as to the meaning of the blurring of the lines in the spectrum, and that you will no longer contend that my letter in *The Times* was based upon a delusion.'

For once our pugnacious colleague was deaf to a challenge. He could but sit gasping and stretching his long, thin limbs, as if to assure himself that he was still really upon this planet. Challenger walked across to the oxygen tube, and the sound of the loud hissing fell away till it was the most gentle sibilation.

'We must husband our supply of the gas,' said he. 'The atmosphere of the room is now strongly hyper-oxygenated, and I take it that none of us feel any distressing symptoms. We can only determine by actual experiments what amount added to the air will serve to neutralise the poison. Let us see how that will do.'

We sat in silent nervous tension for five minutes or more, observing our own sensations. I had just begun to fancy that I felt the constriction round my temples again when Mrs Challenger called out from the sofa that she was fainting. Her husband turned on more gas.

'In pre-scientific days,' said he, 'they used to keep a white mouse in every submarine, as its more delicate organisation gave signs of a vicious atmosphere before it was perceived by the sailors. You, my dear, will be our white mouse. I have now increased the supply and you are better.'

'Yes, I am better.'

'Possibly we have hit upon the correct mixture. When we have ascertained exactly how little will serve we shall be able to compute how long we shall be able to exist. Unfortunately, in resuscitating ourselves we have already consumed a considerable pro-portion of this first tube.'

'Does it matter?' asked Lord John, who was standing with his hands in his pockets close to the window. 'If we have to go, what is the use of holdin' on? You don't suppose there's any chance for us?'

Challenger smiled and shook his head.

'Well, then, don't you think there is more dignity in takin' the jump and not waitin' to be pushed in? If it must be so I'm for sayin' our prayers, turnin' off the gas, and openin' the window.'

'Why not?' said the lady, bravely. 'Surely, George, Lord John is right and it is better so.'

'I most strongly object,' cried Summerlee, in a querulous voice. 'When we must die let us by all means die; but to deliberately anticipate death seems to me to be a foolish and unjustifiable action.'

'What does our young friend say to it?' asked Challenger.

'I think we should see it to the end.'

'And I am strongly of the same opinion,' said he.

'Then, George, if you say so, I think so too,' cried the lady.

'Well, well, I'm only puttin' it as an argument,' said Lord John. 'If you all want to see it through I am with you. It's dooced interestin', and no mistake about that. I've had my share of adventures in my life, and as many thrills as most folk, but I'm endin' on my top note.'

'Granting the continuity of life,' said Challenger.

'A large assumption!' cried Summerlee.

Challenger stared at him in silent reproof.

'Granting the continuity of life,' said he, in his most didactic manner, 'none of us can predicate what opportunities of observation one may have from what we may call the spirit plane to the plane of matter. It surely must be evident to the most obtuse person' (here he glared at Summerlee) 'that it is while we are ourselves material that we are most fitted to watch and form a judgment upon material phenomena. Therefore it is only by keeping alive for these few extra hours that we can hope to carry on with us to some future existence a clear conception of the most stupendous event that the world, or the universe so far as we know it, has ever encountered. To me it would seem a deplorable thing that we should in any way curtail by so much as a minute so wonderful an experience.'

'I am strongly of the same opinion,' cried Summerlee.

'Carried without a division,' said Lord John. 'By George, that poor devil of a chauffeur of yours down in the yard has made his last journey. No use makin' a sally and bringin' him in?'

'It would be absolute madness,' cried Summerlee.

'Well, I suppose it would,' said Lord John. 'It couldn't help him and would scatter our gas all over the house, even if we ever got back alive. My word, look at the little birds under the trees!'

We drew four chairs up to the long, low

window, the lady still resting with closed eyes upon the settee. I remember that the monstrous and grotesque idea crossed my mind — the illusion may have been heightened by the heavy stuffiness of the air which we were breathing — that we were in four front seats of the stalls at the last act of the drama of the world.

In the immediate foreground, beneath our very eyes, was the small yard with the half-cleaned motorcar standing in it. Austin, the chauffeur, had received his final notice at last, for he was sprawling beside the wheel, with a great black bruise upon his forehead where it had struck the step or mudguard in falling. He still held in his hand the nozzle of the hose with which he had been washing down his machine. A couple of small plane trees stood in the corner of the yard, and underneath them lay several pathetic little balls of fluffy feathers, with tiny feet uplifted. The sweep of Death's scythe had included everything great and small within its swathe.

Over the wall of the yard we looked down upon the winding road, which led to the station. A group of the reapers whom we had seen running from the fields were lying all pell-mell, their bodies crossing each other, at the bottom of it. Farther up the nurse-girl lay with her head and shoulders propped against the slope of the grassy bank. She had taken the baby from the perambulator, and it was a motionless bundle of wraps in her arms. Close behind her a tiny patch upon the roadside showed where the little boy was stretched. Still nearer to us was the dead cab-horse kneeling between the shafts. The old driver was hanging over the splash-board like some grotesque scarecrow, his arms dangling absurdly in front of him. Through the window we could dimly discern that a young man was seated. The door was swinging open, and his hand was grasping the handle, as if he had attempted to leap forth at the last instant. In the middle distance lay the golf links, dotted as they had been in the morning with the dark figures of the golfers, lying motionless upon the grass of the course, or among the heather which skirted it. On one particular green there were eight bodies stretched where a foursome with its caddies had held to their game to the last. No bird flew in the blue vault of heaven, no man or beast moved upon the vast countryside which lay before us. The evening sun shone its peaceful radiance across it, but there brooded over it all the stillness and the silence of universal death — a death in which we were so soon to join. At the present instant that one frail sheet of glass, by holding in the extra oxygen, which counteracted the poisoned ether, shut us off from the fate of all our kind. For a few short hours the knowledge and foresight of one man could preserve our little oasis of life in the vast desert of death, and save us from participation in the common catastrophe. Then the gas would run low, we too should lie gasping upon that cherry-coloured boudoir carpet, and the fate of the human race and of all earthly life would be complete. For a long time, in a mood which was too solemn for speech, we looked out at the tragic world.

'There is a house on fire,' said Challenger, at last, pointing to a column of smoke which rose above the trees. 'There will, I expect, be many such — possibly whole cities in flames — when we consider how many folk may have dropped with lights in their hands. The fact of combustion is in itself enough to show that the proportion of oxygen in the atmosphere is normal, and that it is the ether which is at fault. Ah, there you see another blaze on the top of Crowborough Hill. It is the golf clubhouse, or I am mistaken. There is the church clock chiming the hour. It would interest our philosophers to know that man-made mechanism has survived the race who made it.'

'By George!' cried Lord John, rising

excitedly from his chair. 'What's that puff of smoke? It's a train.'

We heard the roar of it, and presently it came flying into sight, going at what seemed to me to be a prodigious speed. Whence it had come, or how far, we had no means of knowing. Only by some miracle of luck could it have gone any distance. But now we were to see the terrific end of its career. A train of coal-trucks stood motionless upon the line. We held our breath as the express roared along the same track. The crash was horrible. Engine and carriages piled themselves into a hill of splintered wood and twisted iron. Red spurts of flame flickered up from the wreckage until it was all ablaze. For half an hour we sat with hardly a word, stunned by the stupendous sight.

'Poor, poor people!' cried Mrs Challenger, at last, clinging with a whimper to her husband's arm.

'My dear, the passengers on that train were no more animate than the coals into which they crashed, or the carbon which they have now become,' said Challenger, stroking her hand soothingly. 'It was a train of the living when it left Victoria, but it was driven and freighted by the dead long before it reached its fate.'

'All over the world the same thing must be

going on,' said I, as a vision of strange happenings rose before me. 'Think of the ships at sea — how they will steam on and on, until the furnaces die down, or until they run full tilt upon some beach. The sailing ships, too — how they will back and fill with their cargoes of dead sailors, while their timbers rot and their joints leak, till one by one they sink below the surface. Perhaps a century hence the Atlantic may still be dotted with the old drifting derelicts.'

'And the folk in the coalmines,' said Summerlee, with a dismal chuckle. 'If ever geologists should by any chance live upon earth again they will have some strange theories of the existence of man in carboniferous strata.'

'I don't profess to know about such things,' remarked Lord John, 'but it seems to me the earth will be 'To let, empty,' after this. When once our human crowd is wiped off it, how will it ever get on again?'

'The world was empty before,' Challenger answered, gravely. 'Under laws which in their inception are beyond and above us, it became peopled. Why may the same process not happen again?'

'My dear Challenger, you can't mean that?'

'I am not in the habit, Professor Summerlee, of saying things which I do not mean.

The observation is trivial.' Out went the beard and down came the eyelids.

'Well, you lived an obstinate dogmatist, and you mean to die one,' said Summerlee, sourly.

'And you, sir, have lived an unimaginative obstructionist, and never can hope now to emerge from it.'

'Your worst critics will never accuse you of lacking imagination,' Summerlee retorted.

'Upon my word!' said Lord John, 'It would be like you if you used up our last gasp of oxygen in abusing each other. What can it matter whether folk come back or not? It surely won't be in our time.'

'In that remark, sir, you betray your own very pronounced limitations,' said Challenger severely. 'The true scientific mind is not to be tied down by its own conditions of time and space. It builds itself an observatory erected upon the border line of present, which separates the infinite past from the infinite future. From this sure post it makes its sallies even to the beginning and to the end of all things. As to death, the scientific mind dies at its post working in normal and methodic fashion to the end. It disregards so petty a thing as its own physical dissolution as completely as it does all other limitations upon the plane of matter. Am I right, Professor Summerlee?'

Summerlee grumbled an ungracious assent. 'With certain reservations, I agree,' said he.

'The ideal scientific mind,' continued Challenger — 'I put it in the third person rather than appear to be too self-complacent — the ideal scientific mind should be capable of thinking out a point of abstract knowledge in the interval between its owner falling from a balloon and reaching the earth. Men of this strong fibre are needed to form the conquerors of Nature and the bodyguard of truth.'

'It strikes me Nature's on top this time,' said Lord John, looking out of the window. 'I've read some leadin' articles about you gentlemen controllin' her, but she's gettin' a bit of her own back.'

'It is but a temporary set-back,' said Challenger, with conviction. 'A few million years, what are they in the great cycle of time? The vegetable world has, as you can see, survived. Look at the leaves of that plane tree. The birds are dead, but the plant flourishes. From this vegetable life in pond and in marsh will come, in time, the tiny crawling microscopic slugs which are the pioneers of that great army of life in which for the instant we five have the extraordinary duty of serving as rearguard. Once the lowest form of life has established itself, the final advent of Man is as certain as the growth of the oak from the acorn. The old circle will swing round once more.'

'But the poison?' I asked. 'Will that not nip life in the bud?'

'The poison may be a mere stratum or layer in the ether — a mephitic Gulf Stream across that mighty ocean in which we float. Or tolerance may be established, and life accommodate itself to a new condition. The mere fact that with a comparatively small hyper-oxygenation of our blood we can hold out against it is surely a proof in itself that no very great change would be needed to enable animal life to endure it.'

The smoking house beyond the trees had burst into flames. We could see the high tongues of fire shooting up into the air.

'It's pretty awful,' muttered Lord John, more impressed than I had ever seen him.

'Well, after all, what does it matter?' I remarked. 'The world is dead. Cremation is surely the best burial.'

'It would shorten us up if this house went ablaze.'

'I foresaw the danger,' said Challenger, 'and asked my wife to guard against it.'

'Everything is quite safe, dear. But my head begins to throb again. What a dreadful atmosphere!'

'We must change it,' said Challenger. He bent over his cylinder of oxygen.

'It's nearly empty,' said he. 'It has lasted us some three hours. It is now close on eight o'clock. We shall get through the night comfortably. I should expect the end about nine o'clock tomorrow morning. We shall see one sunrise, which shall be our own.'

He turned on his second tube and opened for half a minute the fanlight over the door. Then as the air became perceptibly better, but our own symptoms more acute, he closed it once again.

'By the way,' said he, 'man does not live upon oxygen alone. It's dinner time and over. I assure you, gentlemen, that when I invited you to my home and to what I had hoped would be an interesting reunion, I had intended that my kitchen should justify itself. However, we must do what we can. I am sure that you will agree with me that it would be folly to consume our air too rapidly by lighting an oil-stove. I have some small provision of cold meats, bread, and pickles, which, with a couple of bottles of claret, may serve our turn. Thank you, my dear — now as ever you are the queen of managers.'

It was indeed wonderful how, with the self-respect and sense of propriety of the British housekeeper, the lady had within a few minutes adorned the central table with a snow-white cloth, laid the napkins upon it, and set forth the simple meal with all the elegance of civilisation, including an electric torch lamp in the centre. Wonderful, also, was it to find that our appetites were ravenous.

'It is the measure of our emotion,' said Challenger, with that air of condescension with which he brought his scientific mind to the explanation of humble facts. 'We have gone through a great crisis. That means molecular disturbance. That in turn means the need for repair. Great sorrow or great joy should bring intense hunger — not abstinence from food, as our novelists will have it.'

'That's why the country folk have great feasts at funerals,' I hazarded.

'Exactly. Our young friend has hit upon an excellent illustration. Let me give you another slice of tongue.'

'The same with savages,' said Lord John, cutting away at the beef. 'I've seen them buryin' a chief up the Aruwimi River, and they ate a hippo that must have weighed as much as a tribe. There are some of them down New Guinea way that eat the late-lamented himself, just by way of a last tidy up. Well, of all the funeral feasts on this earth, I suppose the one we are takin' is the queerest.'

'The strange thing is,' said Mrs Challenger, 'that I find it impossible to feel grief for those who are gone. There are my father and mother at Bedford. I know that they are dead, and yet in this tremendous universal tragedy I can feel no sharp sorrow for any individuals, even for them.'

'And my old mother in her cottage in Ireland,' said I. 'I can see her in my mind's eye, with her shawl and her lace cap, lying back with closed eyes in the old high-backed chair near the window, her glasses and her book beside her. Why should I mourn her? She has passed and I am passing, and I may be nearer her in some other life than England is to Ireland. Yet I grieve to think that that dear body is no more.'

'As to the body,' remarked Challenger, 'we do not mourn over the parings of our nails nor the cut locks of our hair, though they were once part of ourselves. Neither does a one-legged man yearn sentimentally over his missing member. The physical body has rather been a source of pain and fatigue to us. It is the constant index of our limitations. Why then should we worry about its detachment from our psychical selves?'

'If they can indeed be detached,' Summerlee grumbled. 'But, anyhow, universal death is dreadful.'

'As I have already explained,' said Challenger, 'a universal death must in its nature be far less terrible than an isolated one.'

'Same in a battle,' remarked Lord John. 'If you saw a single man lying on that floor with his chest knocked in and a hole in his face it would turn you sick. But I've seen ten thousand on their backs in the Sudan, and it gave me no such feelin', for when you are makin' history the life of any man is too small a thing to worry over. When a thousand million pass over together, same as happened today, you can't pick your own partic'lar out of the crowd.'

'I wish it were well over with us,' said the lady, wistfully. 'Oh, George, I am so frightened.'

'You'll be the bravest of us all, little lady, when the time comes. I've been a blusterous old husband to you, dear, but you'll just bear in mind that G.E.C. is as he was made and couldn't help himself. After all, you wouldn't have had anyone else?'

'No one in the whole wide world, dear,' said she, and put her arms round his bull neck. We three walked to the window, and stood amazed at the sight which met our eyes.

Darkness had fallen and the dead world was shrouded in gloom. But right across the southern horizon was one long vivid scarlet streak, waxing and waning in vivid pulses of life, leaping suddenly to a crimson zenith and then dying down to a glowing line of fire.

'Lewes is ablaze!' I cried.

'No, it is Brighton which is burning,' said Challenger, stepping across to join us. 'You can see the curved back of the downs against the glow. That fire is miles on the farther side of it. The whole town must be alight.'

There were several red glares at different points, and the pile of *debris* upon the railway line was still smouldering darkly, but they all seemed mere pin-points of light compared to that monstrous conflagration throbbing beyond the hills. What copy it would have made for the *Gazette*! Had ever a journalist such an opening and so little chance of using it — the scoop of scoops, and no one to appreciate it? And then, suddenly, the old instinct of recording came over me. If these men of science could be so true to their life's work to the very end, why should not I, in my humble way, be as constant? No human eye might ever rest upon what I had done. But the long night had to be passed somehow, and for me, at least, sleep seemed to be out of the question. My notes would help to pass the weary hours and to occupy my thoughts. Thus it is that now I have before me the notebook with its scribbled pages, written confusedly upon my knee in the dim, waning light of our one electric torch. Had I the literary touch, they might have been worthy of the occasion. As it is, they may still serve to bring to other minds the long-drawn emotions and tremors of that awful night.

# 4

## A Diary of the Dying

How strange the words look scribbled at the top of the empty page of my book! How stranger still that it is I, Edward Malone, who have written them — I who started only some twelve hours ago from my rooms in Streatham without one thought of the marvels which the day was to bring forth! I look back at the chain of incidents, my interview with McArdle, Challenger's first note of alarm in *The Times*, the absurd journey in the train, the pleasant luncheon, the catastrophe, and now it has come to this — that we linger alone upon an empty planet, and so sure is our fate that I can regard these lines, written from mechanical professional habit and never to be seen by human eyes, as the words of one who is already dead, so closely does he stand to the shadowed borderland over which all outside this one little circle of friends have already gone. I feel how wise and true were the words of Challenger when he said that the real tragedy would be if we were left behind when all that is noble and good and beautiful had passed. But of that there can surely be no danger. Already our second tube of oxygen is drawing to an end. We can count the poor dregs of our lives almost to a minute.

We have just been treated to a lecture, a good quarter of an hour long, from Challenger, who was so excited that he roared and bellowed as if he were addressing his old rows of scientific sceptics in the Queen's Hall. He had certainly a strange audience to harangue: his wife perfectly acquiescent and absolutely ignorant of his meaning, Summer-lee seated in the shadow, querulous and critical, but interested, Lord John lounging in a corner somewhat bored by the whole proceeding, and myself beside the window watching the scene with a kind of detached attention as if it were all a dream or something in which I had no personal interest whatever. Challenger sat at the centre table with the electric light illuminating the slide under the microscope which he had brought from his dressing-room. The small vivid circle of white light from the mirror left half of his rugged, bearded face in brilliant radiance, and half in deepest shadow. He had, it seems, been working of late upon the lowest forms of life, and what excited him at the present moment was that in the microscopic slide made up the day before he found the amoeba to be still alive.

'You can see it for yourselves,' he kept repeating, in great excitement. 'Summerlee, will you step across and satisfy yourself upon the point? Malone, will you kindly verify what I say? The little spindle-shaped things in the centre are diatoms, and may be disregarded since they are probably vegetable rather than animal. But at the right-hand side you will see an undoubted amoeba, moving sluggishly across the field. The upper screw is the fine adjustment. Look at it for yourselves.'

Summerlee did so, and acquiesced. So did I, and perceived a little creature which looked as if it were made of ground glass flowing in a sticky way across the lighted circle. Lord John was prepared to take him on trust.

'I'm not troublin' my head whether he's alive or dead,' said he. 'We don't so much as know each other by sight, so why should I take it to heart? I don't suppose he's worryin' himself over the state of *our* health.'

I laughed at this, and Challenger looked in my direction with his coldest and most supercilious stare. It was a most petrifying experience.

'The flippancy of the half-educated is more obstructive to science than the obtuseness of the ignorant,' said he. 'If Lord John Roxton would condescend — '

'My dear George, don't be so peppery,' said his wife, with her hand on the black mane that drooped over the microscope. 'What can it matter whether the amoeba is alive or not?'

'It matters a great deal,' said Challenger, gruffly.

'Well, let's hear about it,' said Lord John, with a good-humoured smile. 'We may as well talk about that as anything else. If you think I've been too offhand with the thing, or hurt its feelin's in any way, I'll apologise.'

'For my part,' remarked Summerlee, in his creaky, argumentative voice, 'I can't see why you should attach such importance to the creature being alive. It is in the same atmosphere as ourselves, so naturally the poison does not act upon it. If it were outside of this room it would be dead, like all other animal life.'

'Your remarks, my good Summerlee,' said Challenger, with enormous condescension (oh, if I could paint that overbearing, arrogant face in the vivid circle of reflection from the microscope mirror!) — 'your remarks show that you imperfectly appreciate the situation. This specimen was mounted yesterday and was hermetically sealed. None of our oxygen can reach it. But the ether, of course, has penetrated to it, as to every other point upon the universe. Therefore, it has survived the poison. Hence, we may argue that every amoeba outside this room, instead of being dead, as you have erroneously stated, has really survived the catastrophe.'

'Well, even now I don't feel inclined to hip-hurrah about it,' said Lord John. 'What does it matter?'

'It just matters this, that the world is a living instead of a dead one. If you had the scientific imagination, you would cast your mind forward from this one fact, and you would see some few millions of years hence — a mere passing moment in the enormous flux of the ages — the whole world teeming once more with the animal and human life which will spring from this tiny root. You have seen a prairie fire, where the flames have swept every trace of grass or plant from the surface of the earth and left only a blackened waste. You would think that it must be for ever desert. Yet the roots of growth have been left behind, and when you pass the place a few years hence you can no longer tell where the black scars used to be. Here in this tiny creature are the roots of growth of the animal world, and by its inherent development, and evolution, it will surely in time remove every trace of this incomparable crisis in which we are now involved.'

'Dooced interestin'!' said Lord John, lounging across and looking through the microscope. 'Funny little chap to hang number one among the family portraits. Got a fine big shirt-stud on him!'

'The dark object is his nucleus,' said Challenger, with the air of a nurse teaching letters to a baby.

'Well, we needn't feel lonely,' said Lord John, laughing. 'There's somebody livin' besides us on the earth.'

'You seem to take it for granted, Challenger,' said Summerlee, 'that the object for which this world was created was that it should produce and sustain human life.'

'Well, sir, and what object do you suggest?' asked Challenger, bristling at the least hint of contradiction.

'Sometimes I think that it is only the monstrous conceit of mankind which makes him think that all this stage was erected for him to strut upon.'

'We cannot be dogmatic about it, but at least without what you have ventured to call monstrous conceit we can surely say that we are the highest thing in Nature.'

'The highest of which we have cognisance.'

'That, sir, goes without saying.'

'Think of all the millions and possibly billions of years that the earth swung empty through space — or, if not empty, at least without a sign or thought of the human race. Think of it, washed by the rain and scorched by the sun, and swept by the wind for those unnumbered ages. Man only came into being yesterday so far as geological time goes. Why, then, should it be taken for granted that all this stupendous preparation was for his benefit?'

'For whose then — or for what?'

Summerlee shrugged his shoulders.

'How can we tell? For some reason altogether beyond our conception — and man may have been a mere accident, a by-product evolved in the process. It is as if the scum upon the surface of the ocean imagined that the ocean was created in order to produce and sustain it, or a mouse in a cathedral thought that the building was its own proper ordained residence.'

I have jotted down the very words of their argument; but now it degenerates into a mere noisy wrangle with much polysyllabic scientific jargon upon each side. It is no doubt a privilege to hear two such brains discuss the highest questions; but as they are in perpetual disagreement plain folk like Lord John and I get little that is positive from the exhibition. They neutralise each other and we are left as they found us. Now the hubbub has ceased, and Summerlee is coiled up in his chair, while Challenger, still fingering the screws of his microscope, is keeping up a continual low, deep, inarticulate growl like the sea after a storm. Lord John comes over to me, and we look out together into the night.

There is a pale new moon — the last moon that human eyes will ever rest upon — and the stars are most brilliant. Even in the clear plateau air of South America I have never seen them brighter. Possibly this etheric change has some effect upon light. The funeral pyre of Brighton is still blazing, and there is a very distant patch of scarlet in the western sky, which may mean trouble at Arundel or Chichester, possibly even at Portsmouth. I sit and muse and make an occasional note. There is a sweet melancholy in the air. Youth and beauty and chivalry and love — is this to be the end of it all? The starlit earth looks a dreamland of gentle peace. Who would imagine it as the terrible Golgotha strewn with the bodies of the human race? Suddenly, I find myself laughing.

'Halloa, young fellah!' says Lord John, staring at me in surprise. 'We could do with a joke in these hard times. What was it, then?'

'I was thinking of all the great unsolved questions,' I answer; 'the questions that we spent so much labour and thought over. Think of Anglo-German competition, for example — or the Persian Gulf that my old chief was so keen about. Whoever would have guessed, when we fumed and fretted so, how they were to be eventually solved?'

We fall into silence again. I fancy that each of us is thinking of friends that have gone before. Mrs Challenger is sobbing quietly, and her husband is whispering to her. My mind turns to all the most unlikely people, and I see each of them lying white and rigid as poor Austin does in the yard. There is McArdle, for example, I know exactly where he is, with his face upon his writing-desk and his hand on his own telephone, just as I heard him fall. Beaumont, the editor, too — I suppose he is lying upon the blue-and-red Turkey carpet which adorned his sanctum. And the fellows in the reporters' room — Macdona and Murray and Bond. They had certainly died hard at work on their job, with notebooks full of vivid impressions and strange happenings in their hands. I could just imagine how this one would have been packed off to the doctors, and that other to Westminster, and yet a third to St Paul's.

What glorious rows of headlines they must have seen as a last vision beautiful, never destined to materialise in printer's ink! I could see Macdona among the doctors — 'Hope in Harley Street' — Mac had always a weakness for alliteration. 'Interview with Mr Soley Wilson.' 'Famous Specialist says 'Never despair!' ' 'Our Special Correspondent found the eminent scientist seated upon the roof, whither he had retreated to avoid the crowd of terrified patients who had stormed his dwelling. With a manner which plainly showed his appreciation of the immense gravity of the occasion, the celebrated physician refused to admit that every avenue of hope had been closed.' That's how Mac would start. Then there was Bond; he would probably do St Paul's. He fancied his own literary touch. My word, what a theme for him! 'Standing in the little gallery under the dome, and looking down upon that packed mass of despairing humanity, grovelling at this last instant before a Power which they had so persistently ignored, there rose to my ears from the swaying crowd such a low moan of entreaty and terror, such a shuddering cry for help to the Unknown, that — ' and so forth.

Yes, it would be a great end for a reporter, though, like myself, he would die with the

91

treasures still unused. What would Bond not give, poor chap, to see 'J.H.B.' at the foot of a column like that?

But what drivel I am writing! It is just an attempt to pass the weary time. Mrs Challenger has gone to the inner dressing-room, and the Professor says that she is asleep. He is making notes and consulting books at the central table, as calmly as if years of placid work lay before him. He writes with a very noisy quill pen which seems to be screeching scorn at all who disagree with him.

Summerlee has dropped off in his chair, and gives from time to time a peculiarly exasperating snore. Lord John lies back with his hands in his pockets, and his eyes closed. How people can sleep under such conditions is more than I can imagine.

Three-thirty a.m. I have just awakened with a start. It was five minutes past eleven when I made my last entry. I remember winding up my watch and noting the time. So I have wasted some five hours of the little span still left to us. Who would have believed it possible? But I feel very much fresher, and ready for my fate — or try to persuade myself that I am. And yet, the fitter a man is, and the higher his tide of life, the more must he shrink from death. How wise and how merciful is that provision of Nature by which his earthly anchor is usually loosened by many little imperceptible tugs, until his consciousness has drifted out of its untenable earthly harbour into the great sea beyond!

Mrs Challenger is still in the dressing-room. Challenger has fallen asleep in his chair. What a picture! His enormous frame leans back, his huge, hairy hands are clasped across his waistcoat, and his head is so tilted that I can see nothing above his collar save a tangled bristle of luxuriant beard. He shakes with the vibration of his own snoring. Summerlee adds his occasional high tenor to Challenger's sonorous bass. Lord John is sleeping also, his long body doubled up sideways in a basket-chair. The first cold light of dawn is just stealing into the room, and everything is grey and mournful.

I look out at the sunrise — that fateful sunrise which will shine upon an unpeopled world. The human race is gone, extinguished in a day, but the planets swing round and the tides rise or fall, and the wind whispers, and all Nature goes her way, down, as it would seem, to the very amoeba, with never a sign that he who styled himself the lord of creation had ever blessed or cursed the universe with his presence. Down in the yard lies Austin with sprawling limbs, his face glimmering white in the dawn, and the hose-nozzle still projecting from his dead hand. The whole of human kind is typified in that one half-ludicrous and half-pathetic figure, lying so helpless beside the machine which it used to control.

★  ★  ★

Here end the notes which I made at the time. Henceforward events were too swift and too poignant to allow me to write, but they are too clearly outlined in my memory that any detail could escape me.

Some chokiness in my throat made me look at the oxygen cylinders, and I was startled at what I saw. The sands of our lives were running very low. At some period in the night Challenger had switched the tube from the third to the fourth cylinder. Now it was clear that this also was nearly exhausted. That horrible feeling of constriction was closing in upon me. I ran across and, unscrewing the nozzle, I changed it to our last supply. Even as I did so my conscience pricked me, for I felt that perhaps if I had held my hand all of them might have passed in their sleep.

The thought was banished, however, by the voice of the lady from the inner room, crying: 'George, George, I am stifling!'

'It is all right, Mrs Challenger,' I answered, as the others started to their feet. 'I have just turned on a fresh supply.'

Even at such a moment I could not help smiling at Challenger, who with a great hairy fist in each eye was like a huge, bearded baby, new wakened out of sleep. Summerlee was shivering like a man with the ague, human fears, as he realised his position, rising for an instant above the stoicism of the man of science. Lord John, however, was as cool and alert as if he had just been roused on a hunting morning.

'Fifthly and lastly,' said he, glancing at the tube. 'Say, young fellah, don't tell me you've been writin' up your impressions in that paper on your knee.'

'Just a few notes to pass the time.'

'Well, I don't believe anyone but an Irishman would have done that. I expect you'll have to wait till little brother amoeba gets grown up before you'll find a reader. He don't seem to take much stock of things just at present. Well, Herr Professor, what are the prospects?'

Challenger was looking out at the great drifts of morning mist which layover the landscape. Here and there the wooded hills rose like conical islands out of this woolly sea.

'It might be a winding-sheet,' said Mrs

Challenger, who had entered in her dressing-gown. 'There's that song of yours, George, 'Ring out the old, ring in the new.' It was prophetic. But you are shivering, my poor dear friends. I have been warm under a coverlet all night, and you cold in your chairs. But I'll soon set you right.'

The brave little creature hurried away, and presently we heard the sizzling of a kettle. She was back soon with five steaming cups of cocoa upon a tray.

'Drink these,' said she. 'You will feel so much better.'

And we did. Summerlee asked if he might light his pipe, and we all had cigarettes. It steadied our nerves, I think, but it was a mistake, for it made a dreadful atmosphere in that stuffy room. Challenger had to open the ventilator.

'How long, Challenger?' asked Lord John.

'Possibly three hours,' he answered, with a shrug.

'I used to be frightened,' said his wife. 'But the nearer I get to it, the easier it seems. Don't you think we ought to pray, George?'

'You will pray, dear, if you wish,' the big man answered, very gently. 'We all have our own ways of praying. Mine is a complete acquiescence in whatever Fate may send me — a cheerful acquiescence. The highest religion and the highest science seem to unite on that.'

'I cannot truthfully describe my mental attitude as acquiescence and far less cheerful acquiescence,' grumbled Summerlee, over his pipe. 'I submit because I have to. I confess that I should have liked another year of life to finish my classification of the chalk fossils.'

'Your unfinished work is a small thing,' said Challenger, pompously, 'when weighed against the fact that my own *magnum opus*, 'The Ladder of Life,' is still in the first stages. My brain, my reading, my experience — in fact, my whole unique equipment — were to be condensed into that epoch-making volume. And yet, as I say, I acquiesce.'

'I expect we've all left some loose ends stickin' out,' said Lord John. 'What are yours, young fellah?'

'I was working at a book of verses,' I answered.

'Well, the world has escaped that, anyhow,' said Lord John. 'There's always compensation somewhere if you grope around.'

'What about you?' I asked.

'Well, it just so happens, that I was tidied up and ready. I'd promised Merivale to go to Tibet for a snow-leopard in the spring. But it's hard on you, Mrs Challenger, when you have just built up this pretty home.'

'Where George is, there is my home. But, oh, what would I not give for one last walk together in the fresh morning air upon those beautiful downs!'

Our hearts re-echoed her words. The sun had burst through the gauzy mists which veiled it, and the whole broad Weald was washed in golden light. Sitting in our dark and poisonous atmosphere that glorious, clean, windswept countryside seemed a very dream of beauty. Mrs Challenger held her hand stretched out to it in her longing. We drew up chairs and sat in a semicircle in the window. The atmosphere was already very close. It seemed to me that the shadows of death were drawing in upon us — the last of our race. It was like an invisible curtain closing down upon every side.

'That cylinder is not lastin' too well,' said Lord John, with a long gasp for breath.

'The amount contained is variable,' said Challenger, 'depending upon the pressure and care with which it has been bottled. I am inclined to agree with you, Roxton, that this one is defective.'

'So we are to be cheated out of the last hour of our lives,' Summerlee remarked, bitterly. 'An excellent final illustration of the sordid age in which we have lived. Well, Challenger, now is your time if you wish to study the subjective phenomena of physical dissolution.'

'Sit on the stool at my knee and give me your hand,' said Challenger to his wife. 'I think, my friends, that a further delay in this insufferable atmosphere is hardly advisable. You would not desire it, dear, would you?'

His wife gave a little groan and sank her face against his leg.

'I've seen the folk bathin' in the Serpentine in winter,' said Lord John. 'When the rest are in, you see one or two shiverin' on the bank, envyin' the others that have taken the plunge. It's the last that have the worst of it. I'm all for a header and have done with it.'

'You would open the window and face the ether?'

'Better be poisoned than stifled.'

Summerlee nodded his reluctant acquiescence, and held out his thin hand to Challenger.

'We've had our quarrels in our time, but that's all over,' said he. 'We were good friends and had a respect for each other under the surface. Goodbye!'

'Goodbye, young fellah!' said Lord John. 'The window's plastered up. You can't open it.'

Challenger stooped and raised his wife, pressing her to his breast, while she threw her arms round his neck.

'Give me that field glass, Malone,' said he, gravely.

I handed it to him.

'Into the hands of the Power that made us we render ourselves again!' he shouted in his voice of thunder, and at the words he hurled the field-glass through the window.

Full in our flushed faces, before the last tinkle of falling fragments had died away, there came the wholesome breath of the wind, blowing strong and sweet.

I don't know how long we sat in amazed silence. Then, as in a dream, I heard Challenger's voice once more.

'We are back in normal conditions,' he cried. 'The world has cleared the poison belt, but we alone of all mankind are saved.'

# 5

## The Dead World

I remember that we all sat gasping in our chairs, with that sweet, wet south-western breeze, fresh from the sea, flapping the muslin curtains and cooling our flushed faces. I wonder how long we sat! None of us afterwards could agree at all on that point. We were bewildered, stunned, semi-conscious. We had all braced our courage for death, but this fearful and sudden new fact — that we must continue to live after we had survived the race to which we belonged — struck us with the shock of a physical blow, and left us prostrate. Then gradually the suspended mechanism began to move once more; the shuttles of memory worked; ideas weaved themselves together in our minds. We saw, with vivid, merciless clearness, the relations between the past, the present, and the future — the lives that we had led and the lives which we would have to live. Our eyes turned in silent horror upon those of our companions and found the same answering look in theirs. Instead of the joy which men might have been expected to feel who had so narrowly escaped an imminent death, a terrible wave of darkest depression submerged us. Everything on earth that we loved had been washed away into the great, infinite, unknown ocean, and here were we marooned upon this desert island of a world, without companions, hopes, or aspirations. A few years' skulking like jackals among the graves of the human race and then our belated and lonely end would come.

'It's dreadful, George, dreadful!' the lady cried, in an agony of sobs. 'If we had only passed with the others! Oh, why did you save us? I feel as if it is we that are dead and everyone else alive.'

Challenger's great eyebrows were drawn down in concentrated thought, while his huge, hairy paw closed upon the outstretched hand of his wife. I had observed that she always held out her arms to him in trouble as a child would to its mother.

'Without being a fatalist to the point of non-resistance,' said he, 'I have always found that the highest wisdom lies in an acquiescence with the actual.' He spoke slowly, and there was a vibration of feeling in his sonorous voice.

'I do *not* acquiesce,' said Summerlee, firmly.

'I don't see that it matters a row of pins whether you acquiesce or whether you don't,' remarked Lord John. 'You've got to take it, whether you take it fightin' or take it lyin' down, so what's the odds whether you acquiesce or not? I can't remember that anyone asked our permission before the thing began, and nobody's likely to ask it now. So what difference can it make what we may think of it?'

'It is just all the difference between happiness and misery,' said Challenger, with an abstracted face, still patting his wife's hand. 'You can swim with the tide and have peace in mind and soul, or you can thrust against it and be bruised and weary. This business is beyond us, so let us accept it as it stands and say no more.'

'But what in the world are we to do with our lives?' I asked, appealing in desperation to the blue, empty heaven. 'What am I to do, for example? There are no newspapers, so there's an end of my vocation.'

'And there's nothin' left to shoot, and no more soldierin', so there's an end of mine,' said Lord John.

'And there are no students, so there's an end of mine,' cried Summerlee.

'But I have my husband and my house, so I can thank Heaven that there is no end of mine,' said the lady.

'Nor is there an end of mine,' remarked Challenger, 'for science is not dead, and this catastrophe in itself will offer us many more absorbing problems for investigation.'

He had now flung open the windows and we were gazing out upon the silent and motionless landscape.

'Let me consider,' he continued. 'It was about three, or a little after, yesterday afternoon that the world finally entered the poison belt to the extent of being completely submerged. It is now nine o'clock. The question is, at what hour did we pass out from it?'

'The air was very bad at daybreak,' said I.

'Later than that,' said Mrs Challenger. 'As late as eight o'clock I distinctly felt the same choking at my throat which came at the outset.'

'Then we shall say that it passed just after eight o'clock. For seventeen hours the world has been soaked in the poisonous ether. For that length of time the Great Gardener has sterilised the human mould which had grown over the surface of His fruit. Is it possible that the work is incompletely done — that others may have survived besides ourselves?'

'That's what I was wonderin',' said Lord John. 'Why should we be the only pebbles on the beach?'

'It is absurd to suppose that anyone besides ourselves can possibly have survived,' said Summerlee, with conviction. 'Consider that the poison was so virulent that even a man who is as strong as an ox, and has not a nerve in his body, like Malone here, could hardly get up the stairs before he fell unconscious. Is it likely that anyone could stand seventeen minutes of it, far less hours?'

'Unless someone saw it coming and made preparation, same as old friend Challenger did.'

'That, I think, is hardly probable,' said Challenger, projecting his beard and sinking his eyelids. 'The combination of observation, inference, and anticipatory imagination which enabled me to foresee the danger is what one can hardly expect twice in the same generation.'

'Then your conclusion is that everyone is certainly dead?'

'There can be little doubt of that. We have to remember, however, that the poison worked from below upwards, and would possibly be less virulent in the higher strata of the atmosphere. It is strange, indeed, that it should be so; but it presents one of those features which will afford us in the future a fascinating field for study. One could imagine, therefore, that if one had to search for survivors one would turn one's eyes with best hopes of success to some Tibetan village or some Alpine farm, many thousands of feet above the sea-level.'

'Well, considerin' that there are no railroads and no steamers you might as well talk about survivors in the moon,' said Lord John. 'But what I'm askin' myself is whether it's really over or whether it's only half-time.'

Summerlee craned his neck to look round the horizon.

'It seems clear and fine,' said he, in a dubious voice; 'but so it did yesterday. I am by no means assured that it is all over.'

Challenger shrugged his shoulders.

'We must come back once more to our fatalism,' said he. 'If the world has undergone this experience before, which is not outside the range of possibility, it was certainly a very long time ago. Therefore, we may reasonably hope that it will be very long before it occurs again.'

'That's all very well,' said Lord John; 'but if you get an earthquake shock you are mighty likely to have a second one right on the top of it. I think we'd be wise to stretch our legs and have a breath of air while we have the chance. Since our oxygen is exhausted we may just as well be caught outside as in.'

It was strange, the absolute lethargy which

had come upon us as a reaction after our tremendous emotions of the last twenty-four hours. It was both mental and physical, a deep-lying feeling that nothing mattered and that everything was a weariness and a profitless exertion. Even Challenger had succumbed to it, and sat in his chair, with his great head leaning upon his hands, and his thoughts far away, until Lord John and I, catching him by each arm, fairly lifted him on to his feet, receiving only the glare and growl of an angry mastiff for our trouble. However, once we had got out of our narrow haven of refuge into the wider atmosphere of everyday life, our normal energy came gradually back to us once more.

But what were we to begin to do in that graveyard of a world? Could ever men have been faced with such a question since the dawn of time? It is true that our own physical needs, and even our luxuries, were assured for the future. All the stores of food, all the vintages of wine, all the treasures of art were ours for the taking. But what were we to *do*? Some few tasks appealed to us at once, since they lay ready to our hands. We descended into the kitchen, and laid the two domestics upon their respective beds. They seemed to have died without suffering, one in the chair by the fire, the other upon the scullery floor.

Then we carried in poor Austin from the yard. His muscles were set as hard as a board in the most exaggerated rigor mortis, while the contraction of the fibres had drawn his mouth into a hard sardonic grin. This symptom was prevalent among all who had died from the poison. Wherever we went we were confronted by those grinning faces, which seemed to mock at our dreadful position, smiling silently and grimly at the ill-fated survivors of their race.

'Look here,' said Lord John, who had paced restlessly about the dining-room whilst we partook of some food, 'I don't know how you fellows feel about it, but for my part, I simply *can't* sit here and do nothin'.'

'Perhaps,' Challenger answered, 'you would have the kindness to suggest what you think we ought to do.'

'Get a move on us and see all that has happened.'

'That is what I should myself propose.'

'But not in this little country village. We can see from the window all that this place can teach us.'

'Where should we go, then?'

'To London!'

'That's all very well,' grumbled Summerlee. 'You may be equal to a forty-mile walk, but I'm not so sure about Challenger, with his stumpy legs, and I am perfectly sure about myself.'

Challenger was very much annoyed.

'If you could see your way, sir, to confining your remarks to your own physical peculiarities, you would find that you had an ample field for comment,' he cried.

'I had no intention to offend you, my dear Challenger,' cried our tactless friend. 'You can't be held responsible for your own physique. If Nature has given you a short, heavy body you cannot possibly help having stumpy legs.'

Challenger was too furious to answer. He could only growl and blink and bristle. Lord John hastened to intervene before the dispute became more violent.

'You talk of walking. Why should we walk?' said he.

'Do you suggest taking a train?' asked Challenger, still simmering.

'What's the matter with the motorcar? Why should we not go in that?'

'I am not an expert,' said Challenger, pulling at his beard, reflectively. 'At the same time, you are right in supposing that the human intellect in its higher manifestations should be sufficiently flexible to turn itself to anything. Your idea is an excellent one, Lord John. I myself will drive you all to London.'

'You will do nothing of the kind,' said Summerlee, with decision.

'No, indeed, George!' cried his wife. 'You only tried once, and you remember how you crashed through the gate of the garage.'

'It was a momentary want of concentration,' said Challenger, complacently. 'You can consider the matter settled. I will certainly drive you all to London.'

The situation was relieved by Lord John.

'What's the car?' he asked.

'A twenty-horse Humber.'

'Why, I've driven one for years,' said he. 'By George!' he added. 'I never thought I'd live to take the whole human race in one load. There's just room for five, as I remember it. Get your things on, and I'll be ready at the door by ten o'clock.'

Sure enough, at the hour named, the car came purring and crackling from the yard with Lord John at the wheel. I took my seat beside him, while the lady, a useful buffer state, was squeezed in between the two men of wrath at the back. Then Lord John released his brakes, slid his lever rapidly from first to third, and we sped off upon the strangest drive that ever human beings have taken since man first came upon the earth.

You are to picture the loveliness of Nature upon that August day, the freshness of the morning air, the golden glare of the summer sunshine, the cloudless sky, the luxuriant green of the Sussex woods, and the deep purple of heather-clad downs. As you looked round upon the many-coloured beauty of the scene all thought of a vast catastrophe would have passed from your mind had it not been for one sinister sign — the solemn, all-embracing silence. There is a gentle hum of life which pervades a closely-settled country, so deep and constant that one ceases to observe it as the dweller by the sea loses all sense of the constant murmur of the waves. The twitter of birds, the buzz of insects, the far-off echo of voices, the lowing of cattle, the distant barking of dogs, roar of trains, and rattle of carts — all these form one low, unremitting note, striking unheeded upon the ear. We missed it now. This deadly silence was appalling. So solemn was it, so impressive, that the buzz and rattle of our motorcar seemed an unwarrantable intrusion, an indecent disregard of this reverent stillness which lay like a pall over and round the ruins of humanity. It was this grim hush, and the tall clouds of smoke which rose here and there over the countryside from smouldering buildings, which cast a chill into our hearts as we gazed round at the glorious panorama of the Weald.

And then there were the dead! At first those endless groups of drawn and grinning faces filled us with a shuddering horror. So vivid and mordant was the impression that I can live over again that slow descent of the Station Hill, the passing by the nurse-girl with the two babes, the sight of the old horse on his knees between the shafts, the cabman twisted across his seat, and the young man inside with his hand upon the open door in the very act of springing out. Lower down were six reapers all in a litter, their limbs crossing, their dead, unwinking eyes gazing upwards at the glare of heaven. These things I see as in a photograph. But soon, by the merciful provision of Nature, the over-excited nerve ceased to respond. The very vastness of the horror took away from its personal appeal. Individuals merged into groups, groups into crowds, crowds into a universal phenomenon which one soon accepted as the inevitable detail of every scene. Only here and there, where some particularly brutal or grotesque incident caught the attention, did the mind come back with a sudden shock to the personal and human meaning of it all.

Above all there was the fate of the children. That, I remember, filled us with the strongest sense of intolerable injustice. We could have wept — Mrs Challenger did weep — when we passed a great Council school and saw the long trail of tiny figures scattered down the road which led from it. They had been dismissed by their terrified teachers, and were speeding for their homes when the poison caught them in its net. Great numbers of people were at the open windows of the houses. In Tunbridge Wells there was hardly one which had not its staring, smiling face. At the last instant the need of air, that very craving for oxygen which we alone had been able to satisfy, had sent them flying to the window. The side walks, too, were littered with men and women, hatless and bonnetless, who had rushed out of the houses. Many of them had fallen in the roadway. It was a lucky thing that in Lord John we had found an expert driver, for it was no easy matter to pick one's way. Passing through the villages or towns we could only go at a walking pace, and once, I remember, opposite the school at Tonbridge, we had to halt for some time while we carried aside the bodies which blocked our path.

A few small, definite pictures stand out in my memory from amid that long panorama of death upon the Sussex and Kentish high roads. One was that of a great, glittering motorcar standing outside the inn at the village of Southborough. It bore, as I should guess, some pleasure party upon their return from Brighton or from Eastbourne. There were three gaily dressed women, all young and beautiful, one of them with a Peking spaniel upon her lap. With them were a rakish-looking elderly man and a young aristocrat, his eyeglass still in his eye, his cigarette burned down to the stub between the fingers of his begloved hand. Death must have come on them in an instant and fixed them as they sat. Save that the elderly man had at the last moment torn out his collar in an effort to breathe, they might all have been asleep. On one side of the car a waiter with some broken glasses beside a tray was huddled near the step. On the other two very ragged tramps, a man and a woman, lay where they had fallen, the man with his long, thin arm still outstretched, even as he had asked for alms in his lifetime. One instant of time had put aristocrat, waiter, tramp, and dog upon one common footing of inert and dissolving protoplasm.

I remember another singular picture, some miles on the London side of Sevenoaks. There is a large convent upon the left, with a long, green slope in front of it. Upon this slope were assembled a great number of school children, all kneeling at prayer. In front of them was a fringe of nuns, and higher up the slope, facing towards them, a single figure whom we took to be the Mother Superior. Unlike the pleasure-seekers in the motorcar, these people seemed to have had warning of their danger, and to have died beautifully together, the teachers and the taught, assembled for their last common lesson.

My mind is still stunned by that terrific experience, and I grope vainly for means of expression by which I can reproduce the emotions which we felt. Perhaps it is best and wisest not to try, but merely to indicate the facts. Even Summerlee and Challenger were crushed, and we heard nothing of our companions behind us save an occasional whimper from the lady. As to Lord John, he was too intent upon his wheel and the difficult task of threading his way along such roads to have time or inclination for conversation. One phrase he used with such wearisome iteration that it stuck in my memory, and at last almost made me laugh as a comment upon the day of doom.

'Pretty doin's! What!'

That was his ejaculation as each fresh tremendous combination of death and disaster displayed itself before us. 'Pretty doin's! What!' he cried, as we descended the Station Hill at Rotherfield, and it was still

'Pretty doin's! What!' as we picked our way through a wilderness of death in the High Street of Lewisham and the Old Kent Road.

It was here that we received a sudden and amazing shock. Out of the window of a humble corner house there appeared a fluttering handkerchief waving at the end of a long, thin human arm. Never had the sight of unexpected death caused our hearts to stop and then throb so wildly as did this amazing indication of life. Lord John ran the motor to the kerb, and in an instant we had rushed through the open door of the house and up the staircase to the second-floor front room from which the signal proceeded.

A very old lady sat in a chair by the open window, and close to her, laid across a second chair, was a cylinder of oxygen, smaller but of the same shape as those which had saved our own lives. She turned her thin, drawn, bespectacled face towards us as we crowded in at the doorway.

'I feared that I was abandoned here for ever,' said she, 'for I am an invalid and cannot stir.'

'Well, madam,' Challenger answered, 'it is a lucky chance that we happened to pass.'

'I have one all-important question to ask you,' said she. 'Gentlemen, I beg that you will be frank with me. What effect will these

116

events have upon London and North-Western Railway shares?'

We should have laughed had it not been for the tragic eagerness with which she listened for our answer. Mrs Burston, for that was her name, was an aged widow, whose whole income depended upon a small holding of this stock. Her life had been regulated by the rise or fall of the dividend, and she could form no conception of existence save as it was effected by the quotation of her shares. In vain we pointed out to her that all the money in the world was hers for the taking, and was useless when taken. Her old mind would not adapt itself to the new idea, and she wept loudly over her vanished stock. 'It was all I had,' she wailed. 'If that is gone I may as well go too.'

Amid her lamentations we found out how this frail old plant had lived where the whole great forest had fallen. She was a confirmed invalid and an asthmatic. Oxygen had been prescribed for her malady, and a tube was in her room at the moment of the crisis. She had naturally inhaled some as had been her habit when there was a difficulty with her breathing. It had given her relief, and by doling out her supply she had managed to survive the night. Finally she had fallen asleep and been awakened by the buzz of our motorcar. As it was impossible to take her on with us, we saw that she had all necessaries of life and promised to communicate with her in a couple of days at the latest. So we left her, still weeping bitterly over her vanished stock.

As we approached the Thames the block in the streets became thicker and the obstacles more bewildering. It was with difficulty that we made our way across London Bridge. The approaches to it upon the Middlesex side were choked from end to end with frozen traffic which made all further advance in that direction impossible. A ship was blazing brightly alongside one of the wharves near the bridge, and the air was full of drifting smuts and of a heavy acrid smell of burning. There was a cloud of dense smoke somewhere near the Houses of Parliament, but it was impossible from where we were to see what was on fire.

'I don't know how it strikes you,' Lord John remarked, as he brought his engine to a standstill, 'but it seems to me the country is more cheerful than the town. Dead London is gettin' on my nerves. I'm for a cast round and then gettin' back to Rotherfield.'

'I confess that I do not see what we can hope for here,' said Professor Summerlee.

'At the same time,' said Challenger, his great voice booming strangely amid the silence, 'it is difficult for us to conceive that out of seven millions of people there is only this one old woman who by some peculiarity of constitution or some accident of occupation has managed to survive this catastrophe.'

'If there should be others, how can we hope to find them, George?' asked the lady. 'And yet I agree with you that we cannot go back until we have tried.'

Getting out of the car, and leaving it by the kerb, we walked with some difficulty along the crowded pavement of King William Street, and entered the open door of a large insurance office. It was a corner house, and we chose it as commanding a view in every direction. Ascending the stair, we passed through what I suppose to have been the boardroom, for eight elderly men were seated round a long table in the centre of it. The high window was open and we all stepped out upon the balcony. From it we could see the crowded City streets radiating in every direction, while below us the road was black from side to side with the tops of the motionless taxis. All, or nearly all, had their heads pointed outwards, showing how the terrified men of the City had at the last moment made a vain endeavour to rejoin their families in the suburbs or the country. Here and there amid the humbler cabs towered the great brass-spangled motorcar of some wealthy magnate, wedged hopelessly among the dammed stream of arrested traffic. Just beneath us there was such a one of great size and luxurious appearance, with its owner, a fat old man, leaning out, half his gross body through the window, and his podgy hand, gleaming with diamonds, out-stretched as he urged his chauffeur to make a last effort to break through the press.

A dozen motorbuses towered up like islands in this flood, the passengers who crowded the roofs lying all huddled together and across each others' laps like a child's toys in a nursery. On a broad lamp pedestal, in the centre of the roadway, a burly policeman was standing, leaning his back against the post in so natural an attitude that it was hard to realise that he was not alive, while at his feet there lay a ragged newsboy with his bundle of papers on the ground beside him. A paper-cart had got blocked in the crowd, and we could read in large letters, black upon yellow, 'Scene at Lord's. County match interrupted.' This must have been the earliest edition, for there were other placards bearing the legend, 'Is it the End? Great Scientist's Warning.' And another, 'Is Challenger Justi-fied? Ominous Rumours.'

Challenger pointed the latter placard out to

his wife, as it thrust itself like a banner above the throng. I could see him throw out his chest and stroke his beard as he looked at it. It pleased and flattered that complex mind to think that London had died with his name and his words still present in their thoughts. His feelings were so evident that they aroused the sardonic comment of his colleague.

'In the limelight to the last, Challenger,' he remarked.

'So it would appear,' he answered, complacently. 'Well,' he added, as he looked down the long vista of the radiating streets, all silent and all choked up with death, 'I really see no purpose to be served by our staying any longer in London. I suggest that we return at once to Rotherfield, and then take counsel as to how we shall most profitably employ the years which lie before us.'

Only one other picture shall I give of the scenes which we carried back in our memories from the dead City. It is a glimpse which we had of the interior of the old church of St Mary's, which is at the very point where our car was awaiting us. Picking our way among the prostrate figures upon the steps, we pushed open the swing door and entered. It was a wonderful sight. The church was crammed from end to end with kneeling figures in every posture of supplication and abasement. At the last dreadful moment, brought suddenly face to face with the realities of life, those terrific realities which hand over us even while we follow the shadows, the terrified people had rushed into those old City churches which for generations had hardly ever held a congregation. There they huddled as close as they could kneel, many of them in their agitation still wearing their hats, while above them in the pulpit a young man in lay dress had apparently been addressing them when he and they had been overwhelmed by the same fate. He lay now, like Punch in his booth, with his head and two limp arms hanging over the ledge of the pulpit. It was a nightmare, the grey, dusty church, the rows of agonised figures, the dimness and silence of it all. We moved about with hushed whispers, walking upon our tiptoes.

And then suddenly I had an idea. At one corner of the church, near the door, stood the ancient font, and behind it a deep recess in which there hung the ropes for the bell-ringers. Why should we not send a message out over London which would attract to us anyone who might still be alive? I ran across, and pulling at the list-covered rope I was surprised to find how difficult it was to swing the bell. Lord John had followed me.

'By George, young fellah!' said he, pulling off his coat. 'You've hit on a dooced good notion. Give me a grip and we'll soon have a move on it.'

But, even then, so heavy was the bell that it was not until Challenger and Summerlee had added their weight to ours that we heard the roaring and clanging above our heads which told us that the great clapper was ringing out its music. Far over dead London resounded our message of comradeship, and hope to any fellow-man surviving. It cheered our own hearts, that strong, metallic call, and we turned the more earnestly to our work, dragged two feet off the earth with each upward jerk of the rope, but all straining together on the downward heave, Challenger the lowest of all, bending all his great strength to the task, and flopping up and down like a monstrous bullfrog, croaking with every pull. It was at that moment that an artist might have taken a picture of the four adventurers, the comrades of many strange perils in the past, whom fate had now chosen for so supreme an experience. For half an hour we worked, the sweat dropping from our faces, our arms and backs aching with the exertion. Then we went out into the portico of the church, and looked eagerly up and down the silent, crowded streets. Not a sound, not a motion, in answer to our summons.

'It's no use. No one is left,' I cried.

'We can do nothing more,' said Mrs Challenger. 'For God's sake, George, let us get back to Rotherfield. Another hour of this dreadful, silent City would drive me mad.'

We got into the car without another word. Lord John backed her round and turned her to the South. To us the chapter seemed closed. Little did we foresee the strange new chapter which was to open.

# 6

## The Great Awakening

And now I come to the end of this extraordinary incident so over-shadowing in its importance, not only in our own small, individual lives, but in the general history of the human race. As I said when I began my narrative, when that history comes to be written this occurrence will surely stand out among all other events like a mountain towering among its foothills. Our generation has been reserved for a very special fate since it has been chosen to experience so wonderful a thing. How long its effect may last — how long mankind may preserve the humility and reverence which this great shock has taught it, can only be shown by the future. I think it is safe to say that things can never be quite the same again. Never can one realise how powerless and ignorant one is, and how one is upheld by an unseen hand, until for an instant that hand has seemed to close and to crush. Death has been imminent upon us. We know that at any moment it may be again. That grim presence shadows our lives, but who can deny that in that shadow the sense of duty, the feeling of sobriety and responsibility, the appreciation of the gravity and of the objects of life, the earnest desire to develop and improve, have grown and become real with us to a degree that has leavened our whole society from end to end? It is something beyond sects and beyond dogmas. It is rather an alteration of perspective, a shifting of our sense of proportion, a vivid realisation that we are insignificant and evanescent creatures, existing on sufferance and at the mercy of the first chill wind from the unknown. But if the world has grown graver with this knowledge it is not, I think, a sadder place in consequence. Surely we are agreed that the more sober and restrained pleasures of the present are deeper as well as wiser than the noisy, foolish hustle which passed so often for enjoyment in the days of old — days so recent and yet already so inconceivable. Those empty lives which were wasted in aimless visiting and being visited, in the worry of great and unnecessary households, in the arranging and eating of elaborate and tedious meals, have now found rest and health in the reading, the music, the gentle family communion which comes from a simpler and saner division of their time. With greater health and greater pleasure they are richer than before, even after they have paid those increased contributions to the common fund which have so raised the standard of life in these islands.

There is some clash of opinion as to the exact hour of the great awakening. It is generally agreed that, apart from the difference of clocks, there may have been local causes which influenced the action of the poison. Certainly, in each separate district the resurrection was practically simultaneous. There are numerous witnesses that Big Ben pointed to ten minutes past six at the moment. The Astronomer Royal has fixed the Greenwich time at twelve past six. On the other hand, Laird Johnson, a very capable East Anglia observer, has recorded six-twenty as the hour. In the Hebrides it was as late as seven. In our own case there can be no doubt whatever, for I was seated in Challenger's study with his carefully-tested chronometer in front of me at the moment. The hour was a quarter-past six.

An enormous depression was weighing upon my spirits. The cumulative effect of all the dreadful sights which we had seen upon our journey was heavy upon my soul. With my abounding animal health and great physical energy any kind of mental clouding was a rare event. I had the Irish faculty of seeing some gleam of humour in every darkness. But now the obscurity was appalling and unrelieved. The others were downstairs making their plans for the future. I sat by the open window, my chin resting upon my hand, and my mind absorbed in the misery of our situation. Could we continue to live? That was the question which I had begun to ask myself. Was it possible to exist upon a dead world? Just as in physics the greater body draws to itself the lesser, would we not feel an overpowering attraction from that vast body of humanity which had passed into the unknown? How would the end come? Would it be from a return of the poison? Or would the earth be uninhabitable from the mephitic products of universal decay? Or, finally, might our awful situation prey upon and unbalance our minds? A group of insane folk upon a dead world! My mind was brooding upon this last dreadful idea when some slight noise caused me to look down upon the road beneath me. The old cab-horse was coming up the hill!

I was conscious at the same instant of the twittering of birds, of someone coughing in the yard below, and of a background of movement in the landscape. And yet I remember that it was that absurd, emaciated, superannuated cab-horse which held my gaze. Slowly and wheezily it was climbing the slope. Then my eye travelled to the driver sitting hunched up upon the box, and finally to the young man who was leaning out of the window in some excitement and shouting a direction. They were all indubitably, aggressively alive!

Everybody was alive once more! Had it all been a delusion? Was it conceivable that this whole poison belt incident had been an elaborate dream? For an instant my startled brain was really ready to believe it. Then I looked down, and there was the rising blister on my hand where it was frayed by the rope of the City bell. It had really been so, then. And yet here was the world resuscitated — here was life come back in an instant full tide to the planet. Now, as my eyes wandered all over the great landscape, I saw it in every direction — and moving, to my amazement, in the very same groove in which it had halted. There were the golfers. Was it possible that they were going on with their game? Yes, there was a fellow driving off from a tee, and that other group upon the green were surely putting for the hole. The reapers were slowly trooping back to their work. The nurse-girl slapped one of her charges and then began to push the perambulator up the hill. Everyone had unconcernedly taken up the thread at the very point where they had dropped it.

I rushed downstairs, but the hall door was open, and I heard the voices of my companions, loud in astonishment and congratulation, in the yard. How we all shook hands and laughed as we came together, and how Mrs Challenger kissed us all in her emotion, before she finally threw herself into the bear-hug of her husband!

'But they could not have been asleep!' cried Lord John. 'Dash it all Challenger, you don't mean to believe that those folk were asleep with their staring eyes and stiff limbs, and that awful death-grin on their faces!'

'It can only have been the condition that is called catalepsy,' said Challenger. 'It has been a rare phenomenon in the past and has constantly been mistaken for death. While it endures the temperature falls, the respiration disappears, the heartbeat is indistinguishable — in fact, it *is* death, save that it is evanescent. Even the most comprehensive mind' — here he closed his eyes and simpered — 'could hardly conceive a universal outbreak of it in this fashion.'

'You may label it catalepsy,' remarked Summerlee, 'but, after all, that is only a name, and we know as little of the result as we do of the poison which has caused it. The most we can say is that the vitiated ether has produced a temporary death.'

Austin was seated all in a heap on the step of the car. It was his coughing which I had heard from above. He had been holding his head in silence, but now he was muttering to himself and running his eyes over the car.

'Young fat-head!' he grumbled. 'Can't leave things alone!'

'What's the matter, Austin?'

'Lubricators left running, sir. Someone has been fooling with the car. I expect it's that young garden boy, sir.'

Lord John looked guilty.

'I don't know what's amiss with me,' continued Austin, staggering to his feet. 'I expect I came over queer when I was hosing her down. I seem to remember flopping over by the step. But I'll swear I never left those lubricator taps on.'

In a condensed narrative the astonished Austin was told what had happened to himself and the world. The mystery of the dripping lubricators was also explained to him. He listened with an air of deep distrust when told how an amateur had driven his car, and with absorbed interest to the few sentences in which our experiences of the sleeping City were recorded. I can remember his comment when the story was concluded.

'Was you outside the Bank of England, sir?'

'Yes, Austin — '

'With all them millions inside and everybody asleep?'

'That was so.'

'And I not there!' he groaned, and turned dismally once more to the hosing of his car.

There was a sudden grinding of wheels upon gravel. The old cab had actually pulled up at Challenger's door. I saw the young occupant step out from it. An instant later the maid, who looked as tousled and bewildered as if she had that instant been roused from the deepest sleep, appeared with a card upon a tray. Challenger snorted ferociously as he looked at it, and his thick black hair seemed to bristle up in his wrath.

'A Pressman!' he growled. Then with a deprecating smile: 'After all, it is natural that the whole world should hasten to know what I think of such an episode.'

'That can hardly be his errand,' said Summerlee, 'for he was on the road in his cab before ever the crisis came.'

I looked at the card: 'James Baxter, London Correspondent, *New York Monitor*.'

'You'll see him?' said I.

'Not I.'

'Oh, George! You should be kinder and more considerate to others. Surely you have learned something from what we have undergone.'

He tut-tutted and shook his big, obstinate head.

'A poisonous breed! Eh, Malone? The worst breed in modern civilisation, the ready tool of the quack and the hindrance of the self-respecting man! When did they ever say a good word for me?'

'When did you ever say a good word to them?' I answered. 'Come, sir, this is a stranger who has made a journey to see you. I am sure that you won't be rude to him.'

'Well, well,' he grumbled, 'you come with me and do the talking. I protest in advance against any such outrageous invasion of my private life.' Muttering and mumbling, he came rolling after me like an angry and rather ill-conditioned mastiff.

The dapper young American pulled out his notebook and plunged instantly into his subject.

'I came down, sir,' said he, 'because our people in America would very much like to hear more about this danger which is, in your opinion, pressing upon the world.'

'I know of no danger which is now pressing upon the world,' Challenger answered, gruffly.

The Pressman looked at him in mild surprise.

133

'I meant, sir, the chances that the world might run into a belt of poisonous ether.'

'I do not now apprehend any such danger,' said Challenger.

The Pressman looked even more perplexed.

'You are Professor Challenger, are you not?' he asked.

'Yes, sir; that is my name.'

'I cannot understand, then, how you can say that there is no such danger. I am alluding to your own letter, published above your name in the London *Times* of this morning.'

It was Challenger's turn to look surprised.

'This morning?' said he. 'No *London Times* was published this morning.'

'Surely, sir,' said the American, in mild remonstrance, 'you must admit that the London *Times* is a daily paper.' He drew out a copy from his inside pocket. 'Here is the letter to which I refer.'

Challenger chuckled and rubbed his hands.

'I begin to understand,' said he. 'So you read this letter this morning?'

'Yes, sir.'

'And came at once to interview me?'

'Yes, sir.'

'Did you observe anything unusual upon the journey down?'

'Well, to tell the truth, your people seemed

134

more lively and generally human than I have ever seen them. The baggage man set out to tell me a funny story, and that's a new experience for me in this country.'

'Nothing else?'

'Why, no, sir, not that I can recall.'

'Well, now, what hour did you leave Victoria?'

The American smiled.

'I came here to interview you, Professor, but it seems to be a case of 'Is this nigger fishing, or is this fish niggering?' You're doing most of the work.'

'It happens to interest me. Do you recall the hour?'

'Sure. It was half-past twelve.'

'And you arrived?'

'At a quarter-past two.'

'And you hired a cab?'

'That was so.'

'How far do you suppose it is to the station?'

'Well, I should reckon the best part of two miles.'

'So how long do you think it took you?'

'Well, half an hour, maybe, with that asthmatic in front.'

'So it should be three o'clock?'

'Yes, or a trifle after it.'

'Look at your watch.'

The American did so, and then stared at us in astonishment.

'Say!' he cried. 'It's run down. That horse has broken every record, sure. The sun is pretty low, now that I come to look at it. Well, there's something here I don't understand.'

'Have you no remembrance of anything remarkable as you came up the hill?'

'Well, I seem to recollect that I was mighty sleepy once. It comes back to me that I wanted to say something to the driver, and that I couldn't make him heed me. I guess it was the heat, but I felt swimmy for a moment. That's all.'

'So it is with the whole human race,' said Challenger to me. 'They have all felt swimmy for a moment. None of them have as yet any comprehension of what has occurred. Each will go on with his interrupted job as Austin has snatched up his hose-pipe or the golfer continued his game. Your editor, Malone, will continue the issue of his papers, and very much amazed he will be at finding that an issue is missing. Yes, my young friend,' he added, to the American reporter, with a sudden mood of amused geniality, 'it may interest you to know that the world has swum through the poisonous current which swirls

136

like the Gulf Stream through the ocean of ether. You will also kindly note for your own future convenience that today is not Friday, August the twenty-seventh, but Saturday, August the twenty-eighth, and that you sat senseless in your cab for twenty-eight hours upon the Rotherfield Hill.'

And 'right here,' as my American colleague would say, I may bring this narrative to an end. It is, as you are probably aware, only a fuller and more detailed version of the account which appeared in the Monday edition of the *Daily Gazette* — an account which has been universally admitted to be the greatest journalistic scoop of all time, which sold no fewer than three-and-a-half million copies of the paper. Framed upon the wall of my sanctum I retain those magnificent headlines:

TWENTY-EIGHT HOURS' WORLD COMA
UNPRECEDENTED EXPERIENCE
CHALLENGER JUSTIFIED
OUR CORRESPONDENT ESCAPES
ENTHRALLING NARRATIVE
THE OXYGEN ROOM
WEIRD MOTOR DRIVE
DEAD LONDON

## REPLACING THE MISSING PAGE
## GREAT FIRES AND LOSS OF LIFE
## WILL IT RECUR?

Underneath this glorious scroll came nine-and-a-half columns of narrative, in which appeared the first, last, and only account of the history of the planet, so far as one observer could draw it, during one long day of its existence. Challenger and Summerlee have treated the matter in a joint scientific paper, but to me alone was left the popular account. Surely I can sing 'Nunc Dimittis.' What is left but anticlimax in the life of a journalist after that!

But let me not end on sensational headlines and a merely personal triumph. Rather let me quote the sonorous passages in which the greatest of daily papers ended its admirable leader upon the subject — a leader which might well be filed for reference by every thoughtful man.

'It has been a well-worn truism,' said *The Times*, 'that our human race are a feeble folk before the infinite latent forces which surround us. From the prophets of old and from the philosophers of our own time the same message and warning have reached us. But, like all oft-repeated truths, it has in time lost something of its actuality and cogency. A lesson, an actual experience, was needed to bring it home. It is from that salutary but terrible ordeal that we have just emerged, with minds which are still stunned by the suddenness of the blow, and with spirits which are chastened by the realisation of our own limitations and impotence. The world has paid a fearful price for its schooling. Hardly yet have we learned the full tale of disaster, but the destruction by fire of New York, of Orleans, and of Brighton constitutes in itself one of the greatest tragedies in the history of our race. When the account of the railway and shipping accidents has been completed, it will furnish grim reading, although there is evidence to show that in the vast majority of cases the drivers of trains and engineers of steamers succeeded in shutting off their motive power before succumbing to the poison. But the material damage, enormous as it is both in life and in property, is not the consideration which will be uppermost in our minds today. All this may in time be forgotten. But what will not be forgotten, and what will and should continue to obsess our imaginations, is this revelation of the possibilities of the universe, this destruction of our ignorant self-complacency, and this demonstration of how narrow is the path of our material existence, and what abysses may lie upon either side of it. Solemnity and humility are at the base of our emotions today. May they be the foundations upon which a more earnest and reverent race may build a more worthy temple.'

# THE DISINTEGRATION
# MACHINE

# The Disintegration Machine

Professor Challenger was in the worst possible humour. As I stood at the door of his study, my hand upon the handle and my foot upon the mat, I heard a monologue which ran like this, the words booming and reverberating through the house: 'Yes, I say it is the second wrong call. The *second* in one morning. Do you imagine that a man of science is to be distracted from essential work by the constant interference of some idiot at the end of a wire? I will not have it. Send this instant for the manager. Oh! you *are* the manager. Well, why don't you manage? Yes, you certainly manage to distract me from work the importance of which your mind is incapable of understanding. I want the superintendent. He is away? So I should imagine. I will carry you to the law courts if this occurs again. Crowing cocks have been adjudicated upon. I myself have obtained a judgement. If crowing cocks, why not jangling bells? The case is clear. A written apology. Very good. I will consider it. *Good*-morning.'

It was at this point that I ventured to make my entrance. It was certainly an unfortunate moment. I confronted him as he turned from the telephone — a lion in its wrath. His huge black beard was bristling, his great chest was heaving with indignation, and his arrogant grey eyes swept me up and down as the backwash of his anger fell upon me.

'Infernal, idle, overpaid rascals!' he boomed. 'I could hear them laughing while I was making my just complaint. There is a conspiracy to annoy me. And now, young Malone, you arrive to complete a disastrous morning. Are you here, may I ask, on your own account, or has your rag commissioned you to obtain an interview? As a friend you are privileged — as a journalist you are outside the pale.'

I was hunting in my pocket for McArdle's letter when suddenly some new grievance came to his memory. His great hairy hands fumbled about among the papers upon his desk and finally extracted a press cutting.

'You have been good enough to allude to me in one of your recent lucubrations,' he said, shaking the paper at me. 'It was in the course of your somewhat fatuous remarks concerning the recent Saurian remains discovered in the Solenhofen Slates. You began a paragraph with the words: 'Professor G. E. Challenger, who is among our greatest living scientists — ' '

'Well, sir?' I asked.

'Why these invidious qualifications and limitations? Perhaps you can mention who these other predominant scientific men may be to whom you impute equality, or possibly superiority to myself?'

'It was badly worded. I should certainly have said: 'Our greatest living scientist,' ' I admitted. It was after all my own honest belief. My words turned winter into summer.

'My dear young friend, do not imagine that I am exacting, but surrounded as I am by pugnacious and unreasonable colleagues, one is forced to take one's own part. Self-assertion is foreign to my nature, but I have to hold my ground against opposition. Come now! Sit here! What is the reason of your visit?'

I had to tread warily, for I knew how easy it was to set the lion roaring once again. I opened McArdle's letter.

'May I read you this, sir? It is from McArdle, my editor.'

'I remember the man — not an unfavourable specimen of his class.'

'He has, at least, a very high admiration for you. He has turned to you again and again when he needed the highest qualities in some investigation. That is the case now.'

'What does he desire?' Challenger plumed himself like some unwieldy bird under the influence of flattery. He sat down with his elbows upon the desk, his gorilla hands clasped together, his beard bristling forward, and his big grey eyes, half covered by his drooping lids, fixed benignly upon me. He was huge in all that he did, and his benevolence was even more overpowering than his truculence.

'I'll read you his note to me. He says:

'Please call upon our esteemed friend, Professor Challenger, and ask for his co-operation in the following circumstances. There is a Latvian gentleman named Theodore Nemor living at White Friars Mansions, Hampstead, who claims to have invented a machine of a most extraordinary character which is capable of disintegrating any object placed within its sphere of influence. Matter dissolves and returns to its molecular or atomic condition. By reversing the process it can be reassembled. The claim seems to be an extravagant one, and yet there is solid evidence that there is some basis for it and that the man has stumbled upon some remarkable discovery.

'I need not enlarge upon the revolutionary character of such an invention, nor of its extreme importance as a potential weapon of war. A force which could disintegrate a battleship, or turn a battalion, if it were only for a time, into a collection of atoms, would dominate the world. For social and for political reasons not an instant is to be lost in getting to the bottom of the affair. The man courts publicity as he is anxious to sell his invention, so that there is no difficulty in approaching him. The enclosed card will open his doors. What I desire is that you and Professor Challenger shall call upon him, inspect his invention, and write for the *Gazette* a considered report upon the value of the discovery. I expect to hear from you tonight.

R. McARDLE'

'There are my instructions, Professor,' I added, as I refolded the letter. 'I sincerely hope that you will come with me, for how can I, with my limited capacities, act alone in such a matter?'

'True, Malone! True!' purred the great man. 'Though you are by no means destitute of natural intelligence, I agree with you that you would be somewhat over-weighted in such a matter as you lay before me. These unutterable people upon the telephone have

147

already ruined my morning's work, so that a little more can hardly matter. I am engaged in answering that Italian buffoon, Mazotti, whose views upon the larval development of the tropical termites have excited my derision and contempt, but I can leave the complete exposure of the impostor until evening. Meanwhile, I am at your service.'

And thus it came about that on that October morning I found myself in the deep level tube with the Professor speeding to the North of London in what proved to be one of the most singular experiences of my remarkable life.

I had, before leaving Enmore Gardens, ascertained by the much-abused telephone that our man was at home, and had warned him of our coming. He lived in a comfortable flat in Hampstead, and he kept us waiting for quite half an hour in his ante-room whilst he carried on an animated conversation with a group of visitors, whose voices, as they finally bade farewell in the hall, showed that they were Russians. I caught a glimpse of them through the half-opened door, and had a passing impression of prosperous and intelligent men, with astrakhan collars to their coats, glistening top-hats, and every appearance of that bourgeois well-being which the successful Communist so readily assumes.

The hall door closed behind them, and the next instant Theodore Nemor entered our apartment. I can see him now as he stood with the sunlight full upon him, rubbing his long, thin hands together and surveying us with his broad smile and his cunning yellow eyes.

He was a short, thick man, with some suggestion of deformity in his body, though it was difficult to say where that suggestion lay. One might say that he was a hunchback without the hump. His large, soft face was like an underdone dumpling, of the same colour and moist consistency, while the pimples and blotches which adorned it stood out the more aggressively against the pallid background. His eyes were those of a cat, and catlike was the thin, long, bristling moustache above his loose, wet, slobbering mouth. It was all low and repulsive until one came to the sandy eyebrows. From these upwards there was a splendid cranial arch such as I have seldom seen. Even Challenger's hat might have fitted that magnificent head. One might read Theodore Nemor as a vile, crawling conspirator below, but above he might take rank with the great thinkers and philosophers of the world.

'Well, gentlemen,' said he, in a velvety voice with only the least trace of a foreign accent, 'you have come, as I understand from our short chat over the wires, in order to learn more of the Nemor Disintegrator. Is it so?'

'Exactly.'

'May I ask whether you represent the British Government?'

'Not at all. I am a correspondent of the *Gazette*, and this is Professor Challenger.'

'An honoured name — a European name.' His yellow fangs gleamed in obsequious amiability. 'I was about to say that the British Government has lost its chance. What else it has lost it may find out later. Possibly its Empire as well. I was prepared to sell to the first Government which gave me its price, and if it has now fallen into hands of which you may disapprove, you have only yourselves to blame.'

'Then you have sold your secret?'

'At my own price.'

'You think the purchaser will have a monopoly?'

'Undoubtedly he will.'

'But others know the secret as well as you.'

'No, sir.' He touched his great forehead. 'This is the safe in which the secret is securely locked — a better safe than any of steel, and secured by something better than a Yale key. Some may know one side of the matter: others may know another. No one in the world knows the whole matter save only I.'

'And these gentlemen to whom you have sold it.'

'No, sir; I am not so foolish as to hand over the knowledge until the price is paid. After that it is I whom they buy, and they move this safe' — he again tapped his brow — 'with all its contents to whatever point they desire. My part of the bargain will then be done — faithfully, ruthlessly done. After that, history will be made.' He rubbed his hands together and the fixed smile upon his face twisted itself into something like a snarl.

'You will excuse me, sir,' boomed Challenger, who had sat in silence up to now, but whose expressive face registered most complete disapproval of Theodore Nemor, 'we should wish before we discuss the matter to convince ourselves that there is something to discuss. We have not forgotten a recent case where an Italian, who proposed to explode mines from a distance, proved upon investigation to be an arrant impostor. History may well repeat itself. You will understand, sir, that I have a reputation to sustain as a man of science — a reputation which you have been good enough to describe as European, though I have every reason to believe that it is not less conspicuous in America. Caution is a scientific attribute, and you must show us

151

your proofs before we can seriously consider your claims.'

Nemor cast a particularly malignant glance from the yellow eyes at my companion, but the smile of affected geniality broadened upon his face.

'You live up to your reputation, Professor. I had always heard that you were the last man in the world who could be deceived. I am prepared to give you an actual demonstration which cannot fail to convince you, but before we proceed to that I must say a few words upon the general principle.

'You will realise that the experimental plant which I have erected here in my laboratory is a mere model, though within its limits it acts most admirably. There would be no possible difficulty, for example, in disintegrating you and reassembling you, but it is not for such a purpose as that that a great Government is prepared to pay a price which runs into millions. My model is a mere scientific toy. It is only when the same force is invoked upon a large scale that enormous practical effects could be achieved.'

'May we see this model?'

'You will not only see it, Professor Challenger, but you will have the most conclusive demonstration possible upon your own person, if you have the courage to submit to it.'

'If!' the lion began to roar. 'Your 'if', sir, is in the highest degree offensive.'

'Well, well. I had no intention to dispute your courage. I will only say that I will give you an opportunity to demonstrate it. But I would first say a few words upon the underlying laws which govern the matter.

'When certain crystals, salt, for example, or sugar, are placed in water they dissolve and disappear. You would not know that they have ever been there. Then by evaporation or otherwise you lessen the amount of water, and lo! there are your crystals again, visible once more and the same as before. Can you conceive a process by which you, an organic being, are in the same way dissolved into the cosmos, and then by a subtle reversal of the conditions reassembled once more?'

'The analogy is a false one,' cried Challenger. 'Even if I make so monstrous an admission as that our molecules could be dispersed by some disrupting power, why should they reassemble in exactly the same order as before?'

'The objection is an obvious one, and I can only answer that they do so reassemble down to the last atom of the structure. There is an invisible framework and every brick flies into its true place. You may smile, Professor, but your incredulity and your smile may soon be

153

replaced by quite another emotion.'

Challenger shrugged his shoulders. 'I am quite ready to submit it to the test.'

'There is another case which I would impress upon you, gentlemen, and which may help you to grasp the idea. You have heard both in Oriental magic and in Western occultism of the phenomenon of the *apport* when some object is suddenly brought from a distance and appears in a new place. How can such a thing be done save by the loosening of the molecules, their conveyance upon an etheric wave, and their reassembling, each exactly in its own place, drawn together by some irresistible law? That seems a fair analogy to that which is done by my machine.'

'You cannot explain one incredible thing by quoting another incredible thing,' said Challenger. 'I do not believe in your apports, Mr Nemor, and I do not believe in your machine. My time is valuable, and if we are to have any sort of a demonstration I would beg you to proceed with it without further ceremony.'

'Then you will be pleased to follow me,' said the inventor. He led us down the stair of the flat and across a small garden which lay behind. There was a considerable outhouse, which he unlocked and we entered.

Inside was a large whitewashed room with

innumerable copper wires hanging in festoons from the ceiling, and a huge magnet balanced upon a pedestal. In front of this was what looked like a prism of glass, three feet in length and about a foot in diameter. To the right of it was a chair which rested upon a platform of zinc, and which had a burnished copper cap suspended above it. Both the cap and the chair had heavy wires attached to them, and at the side was a sort of ratchet with numbered slots and a handle covered with india-rubber which lay at present in the slot marked zero.

'Nemor's Disintegrator,' said this strange man, waving his hand towards the machine.

'This is the model which is destined to be famous, as altering the balance of power among the nations. Who holds this rules the world. Now, Professor Challenger, you have, if I may say so, treated me with some lack of courtesy and consideration in this matter. Will you dare to sit upon that chair and to allow me to demonstrate upon your own body the capabilities of the new force?'

Challenger had the courage of a lion, and anything in the nature of a defiance roused him in an instant to a frenzy. He rushed at the machine, but I seized his arm and held him back.

'You shall not go,' I said. 'Your life is too

155

valuable. It is monstrous. What possible guarantee of safety have you? The nearest approach to that apparatus which I have ever seen was the electrocution chair at Sing Sing.'

'My guarantee of safety,' said Challenger, 'is that you are a witness and that this person would certainly be held for manslaughter at the least should anything befall me.'

'That would be a poor consolation to the world of science, when you would leave work unfinished which none but you can do. Let me, at least, go first, and then, when the experience proves to be harmless, you can follow.'

Personal danger would never have moved Challenger, but the idea that his scientific work might remain unfinished hit him hard. He hesitated, and before he could make up his mind I had dashed forward and jumped into the chair. I saw the inventor put his hand to the handle. I was aware of a click. Then for a moment there was a sensation of confusion and a mist before my eyes. When they cleared, the inventor with his odious smile was standing before me, and Challenger, with his apple-red cheeks drained of blood and colour, was staring over his shoulder.

'Well, get on with it!' said I.

'It is all over. You responded admirably,' Nemor replied. 'Step out, and Professor

Challenger will now, no doubt, be ready to take his turn.'

I have never seen my old friend so utterly upset. His iron nerve had for a moment completely failed him. He grasped my arm with a shaking hand.

'My God, Malone, it is true,' said he. 'You vanished. There is not a doubt of it. There was a mist for an instant and then vacancy.'

'How long was I away?'

'Two or three minutes. I was, I confess, horrified. I could not imagine that you would return. Then he clicked this lever, if it is a lever, into a new slot and there you were upon the chair, looking a little bewildered but otherwise the same as ever. I thanked God at the sight of you!' He mopped his moist brow with his big red handkerchief.

'Now, sir,' said the inventor. 'Or perhaps your nerve has failed you?'

Challenger visibly braced himself. Then, pushing my protesting hand to one side, he seated himself upon the chair. The handle clicked into number three. He was gone.

I should have been horrified but for the perfect coolness of the operator. 'It is an interesting process, is it not?' he remarked. 'When one considers the tremendous individuality of the Professor it is strange to think that he is at present a molecular cloud suspended in some portion of this building. He is now, of course, entirely at my mercy. If I choose to leave him in suspension there is nothing on earth to prevent me.'

'I would very soon find means to prevent you.'

The smile once again became a snarl. 'You cannot imagine that such a thought ever entered my mind. Good heavens! Think of the permanent dissolution of the great Professor Challenger — vanished into cosmic space and left no trace! Terrible! Terrible! At the same time he has not been as courteous as he might. Don't you think some small lesson — ?'

'No, I do not.'

'Well, we will call it a curious demonstration. Something that would make an interesting paragraph in your paper. For example, I have discovered that the hair of the body being on an entirely different vibration to the living organic tissues can be included or excluded at will. It would interest me to see the bear without his bristles. Behold him!'

There was the click of the lever. An instant later Challenger was seated upon the chair once more. But what a Challenger! What a shorn lion! Furious as I was at the trick that had been played upon him I could hardly keep from roaring with laughter.

His huge head was as bald as a baby's and his chin was as smooth as a girl's. Bereft of his glorious mane the lower part of his face was heavily jowled and ham-shaped, while his whole appearance was that of an old fighting gladiator, battered and bulging, with the jaws of a bulldog over a massive chin.

It may have been some look upon our faces — I have no doubt that the evil grin of my companion had widened at the sight — but, however that may be, Challenger's hand flew up to his head and he became conscious of his condition. The next instant he had sprung out of his chair, seized the inventor by the throat, and had hurled him to the ground. Knowing Challenger's immense strength I was convinced that the man would be killed.

'For God's sake be careful. If you kill him we can never get matters right again!' I cried.

That argument prevailed. Even in his maddest moments Challenger was always open to reason. He sprang up from the floor, dragging the trembling inventor with him. 'I give you five minutes,' he panted in his fury. 'If in five minutes I am not as I was, I will choke the life out of your wretched little body.'

Challenger in a fury was not a safe person to argue with. The bravest man might shrink

159

from him, and there were no signs that Mr Nemor was a particularly brave man. On the contrary, those blotches and warts upon his face had suddenly become much more conspicuous as the face behind them changed from the colour of putty, which was normal, to that of a fish's belly. His limbs were shaking and he could hardly articulate.

'Really, Professor!' he babbled, with his hand to his throat, 'this violence is quite unnecessary. Surely a harmless joke may pass among friends. It was my wish to demonstrate the powers of the machine. I had imagined that you wanted a full demonstration. No offence, I assure you, Professor, none in the world!'

For answer Challenger climbed back into the chair.

'You will keep your eye upon him, Malone. Do not permit any liberties.'

'I'll see to it, sir.'

'Now then, set that matter right or take the consequences.'

The terrified inventor approached his machine. The reuniting power was turned on to the full, and in an instant, there was the old lion with his tangled mane once more. He stroked his beard affectionately with his hands and passed them over his cranium to be sure that the restoration was complete.

Then he descended solemnly from his perch.

'You have taken a liberty, sir, which might have had very serious consequences to yourself. However, I am content to accept your explanation that you only did it for purposes of demonstration. Now, may I ask you a few direct questions upon this remarkable power which you claim to have discovered?'

'I am ready to answer anything save what the source of the power is. That is my secret.'

'And do you seriously inform us that no one in the world knows this except yourself?'

'No one has the least inkling.'

'No assistants?'

'No, sir. I work alone.'

'Dear me! That is most interesting. You have satisfied me as to the reality of the power, but I do not yet perceive its practical bearings.'

'I have explained, sir, that this is a model. But it would be quite easy to erect a plant upon a large scale. You understand that this acts vertically. Certain currents above you, and certain others below you, set up vibrations which either disintegrate or reunite. But the process could be lateral. If it were so conducted it would have the same effect, and cover a space in proportion to the strength of the current.'

'Give an example.'

'We will suppose that one pole was in one small vessel and one in another; a battleship between them would simply vanish into molecules. So also with a column of troops.'

'And you have sold this secret as a monopoly to a single European Power?'

'Yes, sir, I have. When the money is paid over they shall have such power as no nation ever had yet. You don't even now see the full possibilities if placed in capable hands — hands which did not fear to wield the weapon which they held. They are immeasurable.' A gloating smile passed over the man's evil face. 'Conceive a quarter of London in which such machines have been erected. Imagine the effect of such a current upon the scale which could easily be adopted. Why,' he burst into laughter, 'I could imagine the whole Thames valley being swept clean, and not one man, woman, or child left of all these teeming millions!'

The words filled me with horror — and even more the air of exultation with which they were pronounced. They seemed, however, to produce quite a different effect upon my companion. To my surprise he broke into a genial smile and held out his hand to the inventor.

'Well, Mr Nemor, we have to congratulate

you,' said he. 'There is no doubt that you have come upon a remarkable property of nature which you have succeeded in harnessing for the use of man. That this use should be destructive is no doubt very deplorable, but Science knows no distinctions of the sort, but follows knowledge wherever it may lead. Apart from the principle involved you have, I suppose, no objection to my examining the construction of the machine?'

'None in the least. The machine is merely the body. It is the soul of it, the animating principle, which you can never hope to capture.'

'Exactly. But the mere mechanism seems to be a model of ingenuity.' For some time he walked round it and fingered its several parts. Then he hoisted his unwieldy bulk into the insulated chair.

'Would you like another excursion into the cosmos?' asked the inventor.

'Later, perhaps — later! But meanwhile there is, as no doubt you know, some leakage of electricity. I can distinctly feel a weak current passing through me.'

'Impossible. It is quite insulated.'

'But I assure you that I feel it.' He levered himself down from his perch.

The inventor hastened to take his place.

'I can feel nothing.'

'Is there not a tingling down your spine?'

'No, sir, I do not observe it.'

There was a sharp click and the man had disappeared. I looked with amazement at Challenger. 'Good heavens! did you touch the machine, Professor?'

He smiled at me benignly with an air of mild surprise.

'Dear me! I may have inadvertently touched the handle,' said he. 'One is very liable to have awkward incidents with a rough model of this kind. This lever should certainly be guarded.'

'It is in number three. That is the slot which causes disintegration.'

'So I observed when you were operated upon.'

'But I was so excited when he brought you back that I did not see which was the proper slot for the return. Did you notice it?'

'I may have noticed it, young Malone, but I do not burden my mind with small details. There are many slots and we do not know their purpose. We may make the matter worse if we experiment with the unknown. Perhaps it is better to leave matters as they are.'

'And you would — '

'Exactly. It is better so. The interesting personality of Mr Theodore Nemor has distributed itself throughout the cosmos, his machine is worthless, and a certain foreign Government has been deprived of knowledge by which much harm might have been wrought. Not a bad morning's work, young Malone. Your rag will no doubt have an interesting column upon the inexplicable disappearance of a Latvian inventor shortly after the visit of its own special correspondent. I have enjoyed the experience. These are the lighter moments which come to brighten the dull routine of study. But life has its duties as well as its pleasures, and I now return to the Italian Mazotti and his preposterous views upon the larval development of the tropical termites.'

Looking back, it seemed to me that a slight oleaginous mist was still hovering round the chair. 'But surely — ' I urged.

'The first duty of the law-abiding citizen is to prevent murder,' said Professor Challenger. 'I have done so. Enough, Malone, enough! The theme will not bear discussion. It has already disengaged my thoughts too long from matters of more importance.'

# WHEN THE WORLD
# SCREAMED

# When the World Screamed

I had a vague recollection of having heard my friend Edward Malone, of the *Gazette*, speak of Professor Challenger, with whom he had been associated in some remarkable adventures. I am so busy, however, with my own profession, and my firm has been so overtaxed with orders, that I know little of what is going on in the world outside my own special interests. My general recollection was that Challenger had been depicted as a wild genius of a violent and intolerant disposition. I was greatly surprised to receive a business communication from him which was in the following terms:

*14 (Bis), Enmore Gardens, Kensington*

SIR — I have occasion to engage the services of an expert in artesian borings. I will not conceal from you that my opinion of experts is not a high one, and that I have usually found that a man who, like myself, has a well-equipped brain can take a sounder and broader view than the man who professes a special knowledge (which, alas, is so often a mere profession), and is therefore limited in his outlook. None the less, I am disposed to give you a trial. Looking down the list of artesian authorities, a certain oddity — I had almost written absurdity — in your name attracted my attention, and I found upon enquiry that my young friend, Mr Edward Malone, was actually acquainted with you. I am therefore writing to say that I should be glad to have an interview with you, and that if you satisfy my requirements, and my standard is no mean one, I may be inclined to put a most important matter into your hands. I can say no more at present as the matter is one of extreme secrecy, which can only be discussed by word of mouth. I beg, therefore, that you will at once cancel any engagement which you may happen to have, and that you will call upon me at the above address at 10.30 in the morning of next Friday. There is a scraper as well as a mat, and Mrs Challenger is most particular.

I remain, Sir, as I began,

GEORGE EDWARD CHALLENGER

I handed this letter to my chief clerk to answer, and he informed the Professor that

Mr Peerless Jones would be glad to keep the appointment as arranged. It was a perfectly civil business note, but it began with the phrase: 'Your letter (undated) has been received.' This drew a second epistle from the Professor:

Sir [he said — and his writing looked like a barbed wire fence] I observe that you animadvert upon the trifle that my letter was undated. Might I draw your attention to the fact that, as some return for a monstrous taxation, our Government is in the habit of affixing a small circular sign or stamp upon the outside of the envelope which notifies the date of posting? Should this sign be missing or illegible your remedy lies with the proper postal authorities. Meanwhile, I would ask you to confine your observations to matters which concern the business over which I consult you, and to cease to comment upon the form which my own letters may assume.

It was clear to me that I was dealing with a lunatic, so I thought it well before I went any further in the matter to call upon my friend Malone, whom I had known since the old days when we both played Rugger for Richmond. I found him the same jolly

Irishman as ever, and much amused at my first brush with Challenger.

'That's nothing, my boy,' said he. 'You'll feel as if you had been skinned alive when you have been with him five minutes. He beats the world for offensiveness.'

'But why should the world put up with it?'

'They don't. If you collected all the libel actions and all the rows and all the police-court assaults — '

'Assaults!'

'Bless you, he would think nothing of throwing you downstairs if you have a disagreement. He is a primitive caveman in a lounge suit. I can see him with a club in one hand and a jagged bit of flint in the other. Some people are born out of their proper century, but he is born out of his millennium. He belongs to the early neolithic or thereabouts.'

'And he a professor!'

'There is the wonder of it! It's the greatest brain in Europe, with a driving force behind it that can turn all his dreams into facts. They do all they can to hold him back for his colleagues hate him like poison, but a lot of trawlers might as well try to hold back the *Berengaria*. He simply ignores them and steams on his way.'

'Well,' said I, 'one thing is clear. I don't

want to have anything to do with him. I'll cancel that appointment.'

'Not a bit of it. You will keep it to the minute — and mind that it *is* to the minute or you will hear of it.'

'Why should I?'

'Well, I'll tell you. First of all, don't take too seriously what I have said about old Challenger. Everyone who gets close to him learns to love him. There is no real harm in the old bear. Why, I remember how he carried an Indian baby with the smallpox on his back for a hundred miles from the back country down to the Madeira river. He is big every way. He won't hurt you if you get right with him.'

'I won't give him the chance.'

'You will be a fool if you don't. Have you ever heard of the Hengist Down Mystery — the shaft-sinking on the South Coast?'

'Some secret coal-mining exploration, I understand.'

Malone winked.

'Well, you can put it down as that if you like. You see, I am in the old man's confidence, and I can't say anything until he gives the word. But I may tell you this, for it has been in the Press. A man, Betterton, who made his money in rubber, left his whole estate to Challenger some years ago, with the provision that it should be used in the interests of science. It proved to be an enormous sum — several millions. Challenger then bought a property at Hengist Down, in Sussex. It was worthless land on the north edge of the chalk country, and he got a large tract of it, which he wired off. There was a deep gully in the middle of it. Here he began to make an excavation. He announced' — here Malone winked again — 'that there was petroleum in England and that he meant to prove it. He built a little model village with a colony of well-paid workers who are all sworn to keep their mouths shut. The gully is wired off as well as the estate, and the place is guarded by bloodhounds. Several pressmen have nearly lost their lives, to say nothing of the seats of their trousers, from these creatures. It's a big operation, and Sir Thomas Morden's firm has it in hand, but they also are sworn to secrecy. Clearly the time has come when artesian help is needed. Now, would you not be foolish to refuse such a job as that, with all the interest and experience and a big fat cheque at the end of it — to say nothing of rubbing shoulders with the most wonderful man you have ever met or are ever likely to meet?'

Malone's arguments prevailed, and Friday morning found me on my way to Enmore

Gardens. I took such particular care to be in time that I found myself at the door twenty minutes too soon. I was waiting in the street when it struck me that I recognised the Rolls-Royce with the silver arrow mascot at the door. It was certainly that of Jack Devonshire, the junior partner of the great Morden firm. I had always known him as the most urbane of men, so that it was rather a shock to me when he suddenly appeared, and standing outside the door he raised both his hands to heaven and said with great fervour: 'Damn him! Oh, damn him!'

'What is up, Jack? You seem peeved this morning.'

'Hullo, Peerless! Are you in on this job, too?'

'There seems a chance of it.'

'Well, you will find it chastening to the temper.'

'Rather more so than yours can stand, apparently.'

'Well, I should say so. The butler's message to me was: 'The Professor desired me to say, sir, that he was rather busy at present eating an egg, and that if you would call at some more convenient time he would very likely see you.' That was the message delivered by a servant. I may add that I had called to collect forty-two thousand pounds that he owes us.'

I whistled.

'You can't get your money?'

'Oh, yes, he is all right about money. I'll do the old gorilla the justice to say that he is open-handed with money. But he pays when he likes and how he likes, and he cares for nobody. However, you go and try your luck and see how you like it.' With that he flung himself into his motor and was off.

I waited with occasional glances at my watch until the zero hour should arrive. I am, if I may say so, a fairly hefty individual, and a runner-up for the Belsize Boxing Club middleweights, but I have never faced an interview with such trepidation as this. It was not physical, for I was confident I could hold my own if this inspired lunatic should attack me, but it was a mixture of feelings in which fear of some public scandal and dread of losing a lucrative contract were mingled. However, things are always easier when imagination ceases and action begins. I snapped up my watch and made for the door.

It was opened by an old wooden-faced butler, a man who bore an expression, or an absence of expression, which gave the impression that he was so inured to shocks that nothing on earth would surprise him.

'By appointment, sir?' he asked.

'Certainly.'

He glanced at a list in his hand.

'Your name, sir? . . . Quite so, Mr Peerless Jones . . . Ten-thirty. Everything is in order. We have to be careful, Mr Jones, for we are much annoyed by journalists. The Professor, as you may be aware, does not approve of the Press. This way, sir. Professor Challenger is now receiving.'

The next instant I found myself in the presence. I believe that my friend, Ted Malone, has described the man in his 'Lost World' yarn better than I can hope to do, so I'll leave it at that. All I was aware of was a huge trunk of a man behind a mahogany desk, with a great spade-shaped black beard and two large grey eyes half covered with insolent drooping eyelids. His big head sloped back, his beard bristled forward, and his whole appearance conveyed one single impression of arrogant intolerance. 'Well, what the devil do *you* want?' was written all over him. I laid my card on the table.

'Ah yes,' he said, picking it up and handling it as if he disliked the smell of it. 'Of course. You are the expert — so-called. Mr Jones — Mr Peerless Jones. You may thank your godfather, Mr Jones, for it was this ludicrous prefix which first drew my attention to you.'

'I am here, Professor Challenger, for a business interview and not to discuss my own name,' said I, with all the dignity I could master.

'Dear me, you seem to be a very touchy person, Mr Jones. Your nerves are in a highly irritable condition. We must walk warily in dealing with you, Mr Jones. Pray sit down and compose yourself. I have been reading your little brochure upon the reclaiming of the Sinai Peninsula. Did you write it yourself?'

'Naturally, sir. My name is on it.'

'Quite so! Quite so! But it does not always follow, does it? However, I am prepared to accept your assertion. The book is not without merit of a sort. Beneath the dullness of the diction one gets glimpses of an occasional idea. There are germs of thought here and there. Are you a married man?'

'No, sir. I am not.'

'Then there is some chance of your keeping a secret.'

'If I promised to do so, I would certainly keep my promise.'

'So you say. My young friend, Malone' — he spoke as if Ted were ten years of age — 'has a good opinion of you. He says that I may trust you. This trust is a very great one, for I am engaged just now in one of the greatest experiments — I may even say *the* greatest experiment — in the history of the world. I ask for your participation.'

'I shall be honoured.'

'It is indeed an honour. I will admit that I should have shared my labours with no one were it not that the gigantic nature of the undertaking calls for the highest technical skill. Now, Mr Jones, having obtained your promise of inviolable secrecy, I come down to the essential point. It is this — that the world upon which we live is itself a living organism, endowed, as I believe, with a circulation, a respiration, and a nervous system of its own.'

Clearly the man was a lunatic.

'Your brain, I observe,' he continued, 'fails to register. But it will gradually absorb the idea. You will recall how a moor or heath resembles the hairy side of a giant animal. A certain analogy runs through all nature. You will then consider the secular rise and fall of land, which indicates the slow respiration of the creature. Finally, you will note the fidgetings and scratchings which appear to our Lilliputian perceptions as earthquakes and convulsions.'

'What about volcanoes?' I asked.

'Tut, tut! They correspond to the heat spots upon our own bodies.'

My brain whirled as I tried to find some answer to these monstrous contentions.

'The temperature!' I cried. 'Is it not a fact

that it rises rapidly as one descends, and that the centre of the earth is liquid heat?'

He waved my assertion aside.

'You are probably aware, sir, since Council schools are now compulsory, that the earth is flattened at the poles. This means that the pole is nearer to the centre than any other point and would therefore be most affected by this heat of which you spoke. It is notorious, of course, that the conditions of the poles are tropical, is it not?'

'The whole idea is utterly new to me.'

'Of course it is. It is the privilege of the original thinker to put forward ideas which are new and usually unwelcome to the common clay. Now, sir, what is this?' He held up a small object which he had picked from the table.

'I should say it is a sea-urchin.'

'Exactly!' he cried, with an air of exaggerated surprise, as when an infant has done something clever. 'It is a sea-urchin — a common echinus. Nature repeats itself in many forms regardless of the size. This echinus is a model, a prototype, of the world. You perceive that it is roughly circular, but flattened at the poles. Let us then regard the world as a huge echinus. What are your objections?'

My chief objection was that the thing was

too absurd for argument, but I did not dare to say so. I fished around for some less sweeping assertion.

'A living creature needs food,' I said. 'Where could the world sustain its huge bulk?'

'An excellent point — excellent!' said the Professor, with a huge air of patronage. 'You have a quick eye for the obvious, though you are slow in realising the more subtle implications. How does the world get nourishment? Again we turn to our little friends the echinus. The water which surrounds it flows through the tubes of this small creature and provides its nutrition.'

'Then you think that the water — '

'No, sir. The ether. The earth browses upon a circular path in the fields of space, and as it moves the ether is continually pouring through it and providing its vitality. Quite a flock of other little world-echini are doing the same thing, Venus, Mars, and the rest, each with its own field for grazing.'

The man was clearly mad, but there was no arguing with him. He accepted my silence as agreement and smiled at me in most beneficent fashion.

'We are coming on, I perceive,' said he. 'Light is beginning to break in. A little dazzling at first, no doubt, but we will soon

181

get used to it. Pray give me your attention while I found one or two more observations upon this little creature in my hand.

'We will suppose that on this outer hard rind there were certain infinitely small insects which crawled upon the surface. Would the echinus ever be aware of their existence?'

'I should say not.'

'You can well imagine then, that the earth has not the least idea of the way in which it is utilised by the human race. It is quite unaware of this fungus growth of vegetation and evolution of tiny animalcules which has collected upon it during its travels round the sun as barnacles gather upon the ancient vessel. That is the present state of affairs, and that is what I propose to alter.'

I stared in amazement. 'You propose to alter it?'

'I propose to let the earth know that there is at least one person, George Edward Challenger, who calls for attention — who, indeed, insists upon attention. It is certainly the first intimation it has ever had of the sort.'

'And how, sir, will you do this?'

'Ah, there we get down to business. You have touched the spot. I will again call your attention to this interesting little creature which I hold in my hand. It is all nerves and sensibility beneath that protective crust. Is it not evident that if a parasitic animalcule desired to call its attention it would sink a hole in its shell and so stimulate its sensory apparatus?'

'Certainly.'

'Or, again, we will take the case of the homely flea or a mosquito which explores the surface of the human body. We may be unaware of its presence. But presently, when it sinks its proboscis through the skin, which is our crust, we are disagreeably reminded that we are not altogether alone. My plans now will no doubt begin to dawn upon you. Light breaks in the darkness.'

'Good heavens! You propose to sink a shaft through the earth's crust?'

He closed his eyes with ineffable complacency.

'You see before you,' he said, 'the first who will ever pierce that horny hide. I may even put it in the present tense and say who *has* pierced it.'

'You have done it!'

'With the very efficient aid of Morden and Co., I think I may say that I have done it. Several years of constant work which has been carried on night and day, and conducted by every known species of drill, borer, crusher, and explosive, has at last brought us to our goal.'

'You don't mean to say you are through the crust!'

'If your expressions denote bewilderment they may pass. If they denote incredulity — '

'No, sir, nothing of the kind.'

'You will accept my statement without question. We are through the crust. It was exactly fourteen thousand four hundred and forty-two yards thick, or roughly eight miles. In the course of our sinking it may interest you to know that we have exposed a fortune in the matter of coal-beds which would probably in the long run defray the cost of the enterprise. Our chief difficulty has been the springs of water in the lower chalk and Hastings sands, but these we have overcome. The last stage has now been reached — and the last stage is none other than Mr Peerless Jones. You, sir, represent the mosquito. Your artesian borer takes the place of the stinging proboscis. The brain has done its work. Exit the thinker. Enter the mechanical one, the peerless one, with his rod of metal. Do I make myself clear?'

'You talk of eight miles!' I cried. 'Are you aware, sir, that five thousand feet is considered nearly the limit for artesian borings? I am acquainted with one in upper Silesia which is six thousand two hundred feet deep, but it is looked upon as a wonder.'

'You misunderstand me, Mr Peerless. Either my explanation or your brain is at fault, and I will not insist upon which. I am well aware of the limits of artesian borings, and it is not likely that I would have spent millions of pounds upon my colossal tunnel if a six-inch boring would have met my needs. All that I ask you is to have a drill ready which shall be as sharp as possible, not more than a hundred feet in length, and operated by an electric motor. An ordinary percussion drill driven home by a weight will meet every requirement.'

'Why by an electric motor?'

'I am here, Mr Jones, to give orders, not reasons. Before we finish it may happen — it *may*, I say, happen — that your very life may depend upon this drill being started from a distance by electricity. It can, I presume, be done?'

'Certainly it can be done.'

'Then prepare to do it. The matter is not yet ready for your actual presence, but your preparations may now be made. I have nothing more to say.'

'But it is essential,' I expostulated, 'that you should let me know what soil the drill is to penetrate. Sand, or clay, or chalk would each need different treatment.'

'Let us say jelly,' said Challenger. 'Yes, we

will for the present suppose that you have to sink your drill into jelly. And now, Mr Jones, I have matters of some importance to engage my mind, so I will wish you good-morning. You can draw up a formal contract with mention of your charges for my Head of Works.'

I bowed and turned, but before I reached the door my curiosity overcame me. He was already writing furiously with a quill pen screeching over the paper, and he looked up angrily at my interruption.

'Well, sir, what now? I had hoped you were gone.'

'I only wished to ask you, sir, what the object of so extraordinary an experiment can be?'

'Away, sir, away!' he cried, angrily. 'Raise your mind above the base mercantile and utilitarian needs of commerce. Shake off your paltry standards of business. Science seeks knowledge. Let the knowledge lead us where it will, we still must seek it. To know once for all what we are, why we are, where we are, is that not in itself the greatest of all human aspirations? Away, sir, away!'

His great black head was bowed over his papers once more and blended with his beard. The quill pen screeched more shrilly than ever. So I left him, this extraordinary man, with my head in a whirl at the thought of the strange business in which I now found myself to be his partner.

When I got back to my office I found Ted Malone waiting with a broad grin upon his face to know the result of my interview.

'Well!' he cried. 'None the worse? No case of assault and battery? You must have handled him very tactfully. What do you think of the old boy?'

'The most aggravating, insolent, intolerant, self-opinionated man I have ever met, but — '

'Exactly!' cried Malone. 'We all come to that 'but.' Of course, he is all you say and a lot more, but one feels that so big a man is not to be measured in our scale, and that we can endure from him what we would not stand from any other living mortal. Is that not so?'

'Well, I don't know him well enough yet to say, but I will admit that if he is not a mere bullying megalomaniac, and if what he says is true, then he certainly is in a class by himself. But *is* it true?'

'Of course it is true. Challenger always delivers the goods. Now, where are you exactly in the matter? Has he told you about Hengist Down?'

'Yes, in a sketchy sort of way.'

'Well, you may take it from me that the

whole thing is colossal — colossal in conception and colossal in execution. He hates pressmen, but I am in his confidence, for he knows that I will publish no more than he authorises. Therefore I have his plans, or some of his plans. He is such a deep old bird that one never is sure if one has really touched bottom. Anyhow, I know enough to assure you that Hengist Down is a practical proposition and nearly completed. My advice to you now is simply to await events, and meanwhile to get your gear all ready. You'll hear soon enough either from him or from me.'

As it happened, it was from Malone himself that I heard. He came round quite early to my office some weeks later, as the bearer of a message.

'I've come from Challenger,' said he.

'You are like the pilot fish to the shark.'

'I'm proud to be anything to him. He really is a wonder. He has done it all right. It's your turn now, and then he is ready to ring up the curtain.'

'Well, I can't believe it till I see it, but I have everything ready and loaded on a lorry. I could start it off at any moment.'

'Then do so at once. I've given you a tremendous character for energy and punctuality, so mind you don't let me down. In the meantime, come down with me by rail and I will give you an idea of what has to be done.'

It was a lovely spring morning — May 22nd, to be exact — when we made that fateful journey which brought me on to a stage which is destined to be historical. On the way Malone handed me a note from Challenger which I was to accept as my instructions.

Sir [it ran] Upon arriving at Hengist Down you will put yourself at the disposal of Mr Barforth, the Chief Engineer, who is in possession of my plans. My young friend, Malone, the bearer of this, is also in touch with me and may protect me from any personal contact. We have now experienced certain phenomena in the shaft at and below the fourteen thousand-foot level which fully bear out my views as to the nature of a planetary body, but some more sensational proof is needed before I can hope to make an impression upon the torpid intelligence of the modern scientific world. That proof you are destined to afford, and they to witness. As you descend in the lifts you will observe, presuming that you have the rare quality of observation, that you pass in succession the secondary chalk beds, the coal measures, some Devonian and Cambrian indications, and finally the granite, through which the greater part of our tunnel is conducted. The bottom is now covered with tarpaulin, which I order you not to tamper with, as any clumsy handling of the sensitive inner cuticle of the earth might bring about premature results. At my instruction, two strong beams have been laid across the shaft twenty feet above the bottom, with a space between them. This space will act as a clip to hold up your artesian tube. Fifty feet of drill will suffice, twenty of which will project below the beams, so that the point of the drill comes nearly down to the tarpaulin. As you value your life do not let it go further. Thirty feet will then project upwards in the shaft, and when you have released it we may assume that not less than forty feet of drill will bury itself in the earth's substance. As this substance is very soft I find that you will probably need no driving power, and that simply a release of the tube will suffice by its own weight to drive it into the layer which we have uncovered. These instructions would seem to be sufficient for any ordinary intelligence, but I have little doubt that you will need more, which can be referred to me through our young friend, Malone.

GEORGE EDWARD CHALLENGER

It can be imagined that when we arrived at the station of Storrington, near the northern foot of the South Downs I was in a state of considerable nervous tension. A weather-worn Vauxhall thirty landaulette was awaiting us, and bumped us for six or seven miles over by-paths and lanes which, in spite of their natural seclusion, were deeply rutted and showed every sign of heavy traffic. A broken lorry lying in the grass at one point showed that others had found it rough going as well as we. Once a huge piece of machinery which seemed to be the valves and piston of a hydraulic pump projected itself, all rusted, from a clump of furze.

'That's Challenger's doing,' said Malone, grinning. 'Said it was one-tenth of an inch out of estimate, so he simply chucked it by the wayside.'

'With a lawsuit to follow, no doubt.'

'A lawsuit! My dear chap, we should have a court of our own. We have enough to keep a judge busy for a year. Government, too. The old devil cares for no one. Rex *v.* George Challenger and George Challenger *v.* Rex. A nice devil's dance the two will have from one court to another. Well, here we are. All right, Jenkins, you can let us in!'

A huge man with a notable cauliflower ear was peering into the car, a scowl of suspicion upon his face. He relaxed and saluted as he recognised my companion.

'All right, Mr Malone. I thought it was the American Associated Press.'

'Oh, they are on the track, are they?'

'They today, and *The Times* yesterday. Oh, they are buzzing round proper. Look at that!' He indicated a distant dot upon the skyline. 'See that glint! That's the telescope of the Chicago *Daily News*. Yes, they are fair after us now. I've seen 'em in rows, same as the crows, along the Beacon yonder.'

'Poor old Press gang!' said Malone, as we entered a gate in a formidable barbed wire fence. 'I am one of them myself, and I know how it feels.'

At this moment we heard a plaintive bleat behind us of 'Malone! Ted Malone!' It came from a fat little man who had just arrived upon a motorbike and was at present struggling in the Herculean grasp of the gatekeeper.

'Here, let me go!' he sputtered. 'Keep your hands off! Malone, call off this gorilla of yours.'

'Let him go, Jenkins! He's a friend of mine!' cried Malone. 'Well, old bean, what is it? What are you after in these parts? Fleet Street is your stamping ground — not the wilds of Sussex.'

'You know what I am after perfectly well,' said our visitor. 'I've got the assignment to write a story about Hengist Down and I can't go home without the copy.'

'Sorry, Roy, but you can't get anything here. You'll have to stay on that side of the wire. If you want more you must go and see Professor Challenger and get his leave.'

'I've been,' said the journalist, ruefully. 'I went this morning.'

'Well, what did he say?'

'He said he would put me through the window.'

Malone laughed.

'And what did you say?'

'I said, 'What's wrong with the door?' and I skipped through it just to show there was nothing wrong with it. It was no time for argument. I just went. What with that bearded Assyrian bull in London, and this Thug down here, who has ruined my clean celluloid, you seem to be keeping queer company, Ted Malone.'

'I can't help you, Roy; I would if I could. They say in Fleet Street that you have never been beaten, but you are up against it this time. Get back to the office, and if you just wait a few days I'll give you the news as soon as the old man allows.'

'No chance of getting in?'

'Not an earthly.'

'Money no object?'

'You should know better than to say that.'

'They tell me it's a short cut to New Zealand.'

'It will be a short cut to the hospital if you butt in here, Roy. Goodbye, now. We have some work to do of our own.

'That's Roy Perkins, the war correspondent,' said Malone as we walked across the compound. 'We've broken his record, for he is supposed to be undefeatable. It's his fat little innocent face that carries him through everything. We were on the same staff once. Now there' — he pointed to a cluster of pleasant red-roofed bungalows — 'are the quarters of the men. They are a splendid lot of picked workers who are paid far above ordinary rates. They have to be bachelors and teetotallers, and under oath of secrecy. I don't think there has been any leakage up to now. That field is their football ground and the detached house is their library and recreation room. The old man is some organiser, I can assure you. This is Mr Barforth, the head engineer-in-charge.'

A long, thin, melancholy man with deep lines of anxiety upon his face had appeared before us.

'I expect you are the artesian engineer,' said he, in a gloomy voice. 'I was told to expect you. I am glad you've come, for I don't mind telling you that the responsibility of this thing is getting on my nerves. We work away, and I never know if it's a gush of chalk water, or a seam of coal, or a squirt of petroleum, or maybe a touch of hell fire that is coming next. We've been spared the last up to now, but you may make the connection for all I know.'

'Is it so hot down there?'

'Well, it's hot. There's no denying it. And yet maybe it is not hotter than the barometric pressure and the confined space might account for. Of course, the ventilation is awful. We pump the air down, but two-hour shifts are the most the men can do — and they are willing lads too. The Professor was down yesterday, and he was very pleased with it all. You had best join us at lunch, and then you will see it for yourself.'

After a hurried and frugal meal we were introduced with loving assiduity upon the part of the manager to the contents of his engine-house, and to the miscellaneous scrap heap of disused implements with which the grass was littered. On one side was a huge dismantled Arrol hydraulic shovel, with which the first excavations had been rapidly made.

Beside it was a great engine which worked a continuous steel rope on which the skips were fastened which drew up the *debris* by successive stages from the bottom of the shaft. In the powerhouse were several Escher Wyss turbines of great horsepower running at one hundred and forty revolutions a minute and governing hydraulic accumulators which evolved a pressure of fourteen hundred pounds per square inch, passing in three-inch pipes down the shaft and operating four rock drills with hollow cutters of the Brandt type. Abutting upon the engine-house was the electric house supplying power for a very large lighting instalment, and next to that again was an extra turbine of two hundred horsepower, which drove a ten-foot fan forcing air down a twelve-inch pipe to the bottom of the workings. All these wonders were shown with many technical explanations by their proud operator, who was well on his way to boring me stiff, as I may in turn have done my reader. There came a welcome interruption, however, when I heard the roar of wheels and rejoiced to see my Leyland three-tonner come rolling and heaving over the grass, heaped up with my tools and sections of tubing, and bearing my foreman, Peters, and a very grimy assistant in front. The two of them set to work at once to unload my stuff and to carry it in. Leaving them at their work, the manager, with Malone and myself, approached the shaft.

It was a wondrous place, on a very much larger scale than I had imagined. The spoil banks, which represented the thousands of tons removed, had been built up into a great horseshoe around it, which now made a considerable hill. In the concavity of this horseshoe, composed of chalk, clay, coal, and granite, there rose up a bristle of iron pillars and wheels from which the pumps and the lifts were operated. They connected with the brick power building which filled up the gap in the horseshoe. Beyond it lay the open mouth of the shaft, a huge yawning pit, some thirty or forty feet in diameter, lined and topped with brick and cement. As I craned my neck over the side and gazed down into the dreadful abyss, which I had been assured was eight miles deep, my brain reeled at the thought of what it represented. The sunlight struck the mouth of it diagonally, and I could only see some hundreds of yards of dirty white chalk, bricked here and there where the surface had seemed unstable. Even as I looked, however, I saw, far, far down in the darkness, a tiny speck of light, the smallest possible dot, but clear and steady against the inky background.

'What is that light?' I asked.

Malone bent over the parapet beside me.

'That's one of the cages coming up,' said he. 'Rather wonderful, is it not? That is a mile or more from us, and that little gleam is a powerful arc lamp. It travels quickly, and will be here in a few minutes.'

Sure enough the pin-point of light came larger and larger, until it flooded the tube with its silvery radiance, and I had to turn away my eyes from its blinding glare. A moment later the iron cage clashed up to the landing stage, and four men crawled out of it and passed on to the entrance.

'Nearly all in,' said Malone. 'It is no joke to do a two-hour shift at that depth. Well, some of your stuff is ready to hand here. I suppose the best thing we can do is to go down. Then you will be able to judge the situation for yourself.'

There was an annexe to the engine-house into which he led me. A number of baggy suits of the lightest tussore material were hanging from the wall. Following Malone's example I took off every stitch of my clothes, and put on one of these suits, together with a pair of rubber-soled slippers. Malone finished before I did and left the dressing-room. A moment later I heard a noise like ten dog-fights rolled into one, and rushing out I found my friend rolling on the ground with his arms round the workman who was helping to stack my artesian tubing. He was endeavouring to tear something from him to which the other was most desperately clinging. But Malone was too strong for him, tore the object out of his grasp, and danced upon it until it was shattered to pieces. Only then did I recognise that it was a photographic camera. My grimy-faced artisan rose ruefully from the floor.

'Confound you, Ted Malone!' said he. 'That was a new ten-guinea machine.'

'Can't help it, Roy. I saw you take the snap, and there was only one thing to do.'

'How the devil did you get mixed up with my outfit?' I asked, with righteous indignation.

The rascal winked and grinned. 'There are always ways and means,' said he. 'But don't blame your foreman. He thought it was just a rag. I swapped clothes with his assistant, and in I came.'

'And out you go,' said Malone. 'No use arguing, Roy. If Challenger were here he would set the dogs on you. I've been in a hole myself, so I won't be hard, but I am watchdog here, and I can bite as well as bark. Come on! Out you march!'

So our enterprising visitor was marched by two grinning workmen out of the compound.

So now the public will at last understand the genesis of that wonderful four-column article headed 'Mad Dream of a Scientist,' with the subtitle 'A bee-line to Australia,' which appeared in *The Adviser* some days later and brought Challenger to the verge of apoplexy, and the editor of *The Adviser* to the most disagreeable and dangerous interview of his lifetime. The article was a highly coloured and exaggerated account of the adventure of Roy Perkins, 'our experienced war correspondent,' and it contained such purple passages as 'this hirsute bully of Enmore Gardens,' 'a compound guarded by barbed wire, plug-uglies, and bloodhounds,' and finally, 'I was dragged from the edge of the Anglo-Australian tunnel by two ruffians, the more savage being a jack-of-all-trades whom I had previously known by sight as a hanger-on of the journalistic profession, while the other, a sinister figure in a strange tropical garb, was posing as an artesian engineer, though his appearance was more reminiscent of Whitechapel.' Having ticked us off in this way, the rascal had an elaborate description of rails at the pit mouth, and of a zigzag excavation by which funicular trains were to burrow into the earth. The only practical inconvenience arising from the article was that it notably increased that line of loafers who sat upon the South Downs waiting for something to happen. The day came when it did happen and when they wished themselves elsewhere.

My foreman with his faked assistant had littered the place with all my apparatus, my bell box, my crow's foot, the V-drills, the rods, and the weight, but Malone insisted that we disregard all that and descend ourselves to the lowest level. To this end we entered the cage, which was of latticed steel, and in the company of the chief engineer we shot down into the bowels of the earth. There were a series of automatic lifts, each with its own operating station hollowed out in the side of the excavation. They operated with great speed, and the experience was more like a vertical railway journey than the deliberate fall which we associate with the British lift.

Since the cage was latticed and brightly illuminated, we had a clear view of the strata through which we passed. I was conscious of each of them as we flashed past. There were the sallow lower chalk, the coffee-coloured Hastings beds, the lighter Ashburnham beds, the dark carboniferous clays, and then, gleaming in the electric light, band after band of jet-black, sparkling coal alternating with the rings of clay. Here and there brickwork had been inserted, but as a rule the shaft was self-supported, and one could but marvel at the immense labour and mechanical skill which it represented. Beneath the coal-beds I was conscious of jumbled strata of a concrete-like appearance, and then we shot down into the primitive granite, where the quartz crystals gleamed and twinkled as if the dark walls were sown with the dust of diamonds. Down we went and ever down — lower now than ever mortals had before penetrated. The archaic rocks varied wonderfully in colour, and I can never forget one broad belt of rose-coloured felspar, which shone with an unearthly beauty before our powerful lamps. Stage after stage, and lift after lift, the air getting ever closer and hotter until even the light tussore garments were intolerable and the sweat was pouring down into those rubber-soled slippers. At last, just as I was thinking that I could stand it no more, the last lift came to a stand and we stepped out upon a circular platform which had been cut in the rock. I noticed that Malone gave a curiously suspicious glance round at the walls as he did so. If I did not know him to be among the bravest of men, I should say that he was exceedingly nervous.

'Funny-looking stuff,' said the chief engineer, passing his hand over the nearest section of rock. He held it to the light and showed that it was glistening with a curious slimy scum. 'There have been shiverings and tremblings down here. I don't know what we are dealing with. The Professor seems pleased with it, but it's all new to me.'

'I am bound to say I've seen that wall fairly shake itself,' said Malone. 'Last time I was down here we fixed those two crossbeams for your drill, and when we cut into it for the supports it winced at every stroke. The old man's theory seemed absurd in solid old London town, but down here, eight miles under the surface, I am not so sure about it.'

'If you saw what was under that tarpaulin you would be even less sure,' said the engineer. 'All this lower rock cut like cheese, and when we were through it we came on a new formation like nothing on earth. 'Cover it up! Don't touch it!' said the Professor. So we tarpaulined it according to his instructions and there it lies.'

'Could we not have a look?'

A frightened expression came over the engineer's lugubrious countenance.

'It's no joke disobeying the Professor,' said he. 'He is so damn cunning, too, that you never know what check he has set on you. However, we'll have a peep and chance it.' He turned down our reflector lamp so that the light gleamed upon the black tarpaulin. Then he stooped and, seizing a rope which connected up with the corner of the covering, he disclosed half-a-dozen square yards of the surface beneath it.

It was a most extraordinary and terrifying sight. The floor consisted of some greyish material, glazed and shiny, which rose and fell in slow palpitation. The throbs were not direct, but gave the impression of a gentle ripple or rhythm, which ran across the surface. This surface itself was not entirely homogeneous, but beneath it, seen as through ground glass, there were dim whitish patches or vacuoles, which varied constantly in shape and size. We stood all three gazing spellbound at this extraordinary sight.

'Does look rather like a skinned animal,' said Malone in an awed whisper. 'The old man may not be so far out with his blessed echinus.'

'Good Lord!' I cried. 'And am I to plunge a harpoon into that beast!'

'That's your privilege, my son,' said Malone, 'and, sad to relate, unless I give it a miss in baulk, I shall have to be at your side when you do it.'

'Well, I won't,' said the head engineer, with decision. 'I was never clearer on anything than I am on that. If the old man insists, then I resign my portfolio. Good Lord, look at that!'

The grey surface gave a sudden heave

upwards, welling towards us as a wave does when you look down from the bulwarks. Then it subsided and the dim beatings and throbbings continued as before. Barforth lowered the rope and replaced the tarpaulin.

'Seemed almost as if it knew we were here,' said he. 'Why should it swell up towards us like that? I expect the light had some sort of effect upon it.'

'What am I expected to do now?' I asked.

Mr Barforth pointed to two beams which lay across the pit just under the stopping place of the lift. There was a interval of about nine inches between them.

'That was the old man's idea,' said he. 'I think I could have fixed it better, but you might as well try to argue with a mad buffalo. It is easier and safer just to do whatever he says. His idea is that you should use your six-inch bore and fasten it in some way between these supports.'

'Well, I don't think there would be much difficulty about that,' I answered. 'I'll take the job over as from today.'

It was, as one might imagine, the strangest experience of my very varied life which has included well-sinking in every continent upon earth. As Professor Challenger was so insistent that the operation should be started from a distance, and as I began to see a good deal of sense in his contention, I had to plan some method of electric control, which was easy enough as the pit was wired from top to bottom. With infinite care my foreman, Peters, and I brought down our lengths of tubing and stacked them on the rocky ledge. Then we raised the stage of the lowest lift so as to give ourselves room. As we proposed to use the percussion system, for it would not do to trust entirely to gravity, we hung our hundred-pound weight over a pulley beneath the lift, and ran our tubes down beneath it with a V-shaped terminal. Finally, the rope which held the weight was secured to the side of the shaft in such a way that an electrical discharge would release it. It was delicate and difficult work done in a more than tropical heat, and with the ever-present feeling that a slip of a foot or the dropping of a tool upon the tarpaulin beneath us might bring about some inconceivable catastrophe. We were awed, too, by our surroundings. Again and again I have seen a strange quiver and shiver pass down the walls, and have even felt a dull throb against my hands as I touched them. Neither Peters nor I were very sorry when we signalled for the last time that we were ready for the surface, and were able to report to Mr Barforth that Professor Challenger could make his experiment as soon as he chose.

And it was not long that we had to wait. Only three days after my date of completion my notice arrived.

It was an ordinary invitation card such as one uses for 'At Homes', and it ran thus:

Professor G. E. Challenger, FRS, MD, D.SC. etc.
(*late President Zoological Institute and holder of so many honorary degrees and appointments that they overtax the capacity of this card*)
requests the attendance of
Mr Jones (no lady) at 11.30 a.m.
of Tuesday, June 21st,
to witness a remarkable triumph of mind over matter at Hengist Down, Sussex
Special train Victoria 10.5. Passengers pay their own fares.
Lunch after the experiment or not — according to circumstances.Station, Storrington.
R.S.V.P. (*and at once with name in block letters*),
14 (*Bis*), Enmore Gardens, London SW

I found that Malone had just received a similar missive over which he was chuckling. 'It is mere swank sending it to us,' said he.

'We have to be there whatever happens, as the hangman said to the murderer. But I tell you this has set all London buzzing. The old man is where he likes to be, with a pin-point limelight right on his hairy old head.'

And so at last the great day came. Personally I thought it well to go down the night before so as to be sure that everything was in order. Our borer was fixed in position, the weight was adjusted, the electric contacts could be easily switched on, and I was satisfied that my own part in this strange experiment would be carried out without a hitch. The electric controls were operated at a point some five hundred yards from the mouth of the shaft, to minimise any personal danger. When on the fateful morning, an ideal English summer day, I came to the surface with my mind assured, I climbed halfway up the slope of the Down in order to have a general view of the proceedings.

All the world seemed to be coming to Hengist Down. As far as we could see the roads were dotted with people. Motorcars came bumping and swaying down the lanes, and discharged their passengers at the gate of the compound. This was in most cases the end of their progress. A powerful band of janitors waited at the entrance, and no promises or bribes, but only the production of the coveted buff tickets, could get them any farther. They dispersed therefore and joined the vast crowd which was already assembling on the side of the hill and covering the ridge with a dense mass of spectators. The place was like Epsom Downs on the Derby Day. Inside the compound certain areas had been wired off, and the various privileged people were conducted to the particular pen to which they had been allotted. There was one for peers, one for members of the House of Commons, and one for the heads of learned societies and the men of fame in the scientific world, including Le Pellier of the Sorbonne and Dr Driesinger of the Berlin Academy. A special reserved enclosure with sandbags and a corrugated iron roof was set aside for three members of the Royal Family.

At a quarter past eleven a succession of charabancs brought up the specially-invited guests from the station and I went down into the compound to assist at the reception. Professor Challenger stood by the select enclosure, resplendent in frock-coat, white waistcoat, and burnished top-hat, his expression a blend of overpowering and almost offensive benevolence, mixed with most portentous self-importance. 'Clearly a typical victim of the Jehovah complex,' as one of his critics described him. He assisted in conducting and occasionally in propelling his guests into their proper places, and then, having gathered the élite of the company around him, he took his station upon the top of a convenient hillock and looked around him with the air of the chairman who expects some welcoming applause. As none was forthcoming, he plunged at once into his subject, his voice booming to the farthest extremities of the enclosure.

'Gentlemen,' he roared, 'upon this occasion I have not need to include the ladies. If I have not invited them to be present with us this morning it is not, I can assure you, for want of appreciation, for I may say' — with elephantine humour and mock modesty — 'that the relations between us upon both sides have always been excellent, and indeed intimate. The real reason is that some small element of danger is involved in our experiment, though it is not sufficient to justify the discomposure which I see upon many of your faces. It will interest the members of the Press to know that I have reserved very special seats for them upon the spoil banks which immediately overlook the scene of the operation. They have shown an interest which is sometimes indistinguishable from impertinence in my affairs, so that on this occasion at least they cannot complain that I have been remiss in studying their convenience. If nothing happens, which is always possible, I have at least done my best for them. If, on the other hand, something does happen, they will be in an excellent position to experience and record it, should they ultimately feel equal to the task.

'It is, as you will readily understand, impossible for a man of science to explain to what I may describe, without undue disrespect, as the common herd, the various reasons for his conclusions or his actions. I hear some unmannerly interruptions, and I will ask the gentleman with the horn spectacles to cease waving his umbrella. (A voice: 'Your description of your guests, sir, is most offensive.') Possibly it is my phrase, 'the common herd', which has ruffled the gentleman. Let us say, then, that my listeners are a most uncommon herd. We will not quibble over phrases. I was about to say, before I was interrupted by this unseemly remark, that the whole matter is very fully and lucidly discussed in my forthcoming volume upon the earth, which I may describe with all due modesty as one of the epoch-making books of the world's history. (General interruption and cries of 'Get down to the facts!' 'What are we here for?' 'Is this a practical joke?') I was about to make the matter clear, and if I have any further interruption I shall be compelled to take means to preserve decency and order, the lack of which is so painfully obvious. The position is, then, that I have sunk a shaft through the crust of the earth and that I am about to try the effect of a vigorous stimulation of its sensory cortex, a delicate operation which will be carried out by my subordinates, Mr Peerless Jones, a self-styled expert in artesian borings, and Mr Edward Malone, who represents myself upon this occasion. The exposed and sensitive substance will be pricked, and how it will react is a matter for conjecture. If you will now kindly take your seats these two gentlemen will descend into the pit and make the final adjustments. I will then press the electric button upon this table and the experiment will be complete.'

An audience after one of Challenger's harangues usually felt as if, like the earth, its protective epidermis had been pierced and its nerves laid bare. This assembly was no exception, and there was a dull murmur of criticism and resentment as they returned to their places. Challenger sat alone on the top of the mound, a small table beside him, his black mane and beard vibrating with excitement, a most portentous figure. Neither

Malone nor I could admire the scene, however, for we hurried off upon our extraordinary errand. Twenty minutes later we were at the bottom of the shaft, and had pulled the tarpaulin from the exposed surface.

It was an amazing sight which lay before us. By some strange cosmic telepathy the old planet seemed to know that an unheard-of liberty was about to be attempted. The exposed surface was like a boiling pot. Great grey bubbles rose and burst with a crackling report. The air-spaces and vacuoles below the skin separated and coalesced in an agitated activity. The transverse ripples were stronger and faster in their rhythm than before. A dark purple fluid appeared to pulse in the tortuous anastomoses of channels which lay under the surface. The throb of life was in it all. A heavy smell made the air hardly fit for human lungs.

My gaze was fixed upon this strange spectacle when Malone at my elbow gave a sudden gasp of alarm. 'My God, Jones!' he cried. 'Look there!'

I gave one glance, and the next instant I released the electric connection and I sprang into the lift. 'Come on!' I cried. 'It may be a race for life!'

What we had seen was indeed alarming. The whole lower shaft, it would seem, had

213

shared in the increased activity which we had observed below, and the walls were throbbing and pulsing in sympathy. This movement had reacted upon the holes in which the beams rested, and it was clear that with a very little further retraction — a matter of inches — the beams would fall. If they did so then the sharp end of my rod would, of course, penetrate the earth quite independently of the electric release. Before that happened it was vital that Malone and I should be out of the shaft. To be eight miles down in the earth with the chance any instant of some extraordinary convulsion taking place was a terrible prospect. We fled wildly for the surface.

Shall either of us ever forget that nightmare journey? The lifts whizzed and buzzed and yet the minutes seemed to be hours. As we reached each stage we sprang out, jumped into the next lift, touched the release and flew onwards. Through the steel latticed roof we could see far away the little circle of light which marked the mouth of the shaft. Now it grew wider and wider, until it came full circle and our glad eyes rested upon the brickwork of the opening. Up we shot, and up — and then at last in a glad mad moment of joy and thankfulness we sprang out of our prison and had our feet upon the green sward once more. But it was touch and go. We had not gone thirty paces from the shaft when far down in the depths my iron dart shot into the nerve ganglion of old Mother Earth and the great moment had arrived.

What was it happened? Neither Malone nor I was in a position to say, for both of us were swept off our feet as by a cyclone and swirled along the grass, revolving round and round like two curling stones upon an ice rink. At the same time our ears were assailed by the most horrible yell that ever yet was heard. Who is there of all the hundreds who have attempted it who has ever yet described adequately that terrible cry? It was a howl in which pain, anger, menace, and the outraged majesty of Nature all blended into one hideous shriek. For a full minute it lasted, a thousand sirens in one, paralysing all the great multitude with its fierce insistence, and floating away through the still summer air until it went echoing along the whole South Coast and even reached our French neighbours across the Channel. No sound in history has ever equalled the cry of the injured Earth.

Dazed and deafened, Malone and I were aware of the shock and of the sound, but it is from the narrative of others that we learned the other details of that extraordinary scene.

The first emergence from the bowels of the earth consisted of the lift cages. The other machinery being against the walls escaped the blast, but the solid floors of the cages took the full force of the upward current. When several separate pellets are placed in a blow-pipe they still shoot forth in their order and separately from each other. So the fourteen lift cages appeared one after the other in the air, each soaring after the other, and describing a glorious parabola which landed one of them in the sea near Worthing pier, and a second one in a field not far from Chichester. Spectators have averred that of all the strange sights that they had ever seen nothing could exceed that of the fourteen lift cages sailing serenely through the blue heavens.

Then came the geyser. It was an enormous spout of vile treacly substance of the consistence of tar, which shot up into the air to a height which has been computed at two thousand feet. An inquisitive aeroplane, which had been hovering over the scene, was picked off as by an Archie and made a forced landing, man and machine buried in filth. This horrible stuff, which had a most penetrating and nauseous odour, may have represented the life blood of the planet, or it may be, as Professor Driesinger and the Berlin School maintain, that it is a protective secretion, analogous to that of the skunk, which Nature has provided in order to defend Mother Earth from intrusive Challengers. If that were so the prime offender, seated on his throne upon the hillock, escaped untarnished, while the unfortunate Press were so soaked and saturated, being in the direct line of fire, that none of them was capable of entering decent society for many weeks. This gush of putridity was blown southwards by the breeze, and descended upon the unhappy crowd who had waited so long and so patiently upon the crest of the Downs to see what would happen. There were no casualties. No home was left desolate, but many were made odoriferous, and still carry within their walls some souvenir of that great occasion.

And then came the closing of the pit. As Nature slowly closes a wound from below upwards, so does the Earth with extreme rapidity mend any rent which is made in its vital substance. There was a prolonged high-pitched crash as the sides of the shaft came together, the sound, reverberating from the depths and then rising higher and higher until with a deafening bang the brick circle at the orifice flattened out and clashed together, while a tremor like a small earthquake shook down the spoil banks and piled a pyramid fifty feet high of *debris* and broken iron over the spot where the hole had been. Professor Challenger's experiment was not only finished, it was buried from human sight for ever. If it were not for the obelisk which has now been erected by the Royal Society it is doubtful if our descendants would ever know the exact site of that remarkable occurrence.

And then came the grand finale. For a long period after these successive phenomena there was a hush and a tense stillness as folk reassembled their wits and tried to realise exactly what had occurred and how it had come about. And then suddenly the mighty achievement, the huge sweep of the conception, the genius and wonder of the execution, broke upon their minds. With one impulse they turned upon Challenger. From every part of the field there came the cries of admiration, and from his hillock he could look down upon the lake of upturned faces broken only by the rise and fall of the waving handkerchiefs. As I look back I see him best as I saw him then. He rose from his chair, his eyes half closed, a smile of conscious merit upon his face, his left hand upon his hip, his right buried in the breast of his frock-coat. Surely that picture will be fixed for ever, for I heard the cameras clicking round me like crickets in a field. The June sun shone golden upon him as he turned gravely bowing to each quarter of the compass. Challenger the super scientist, Challenger the arch pioneer, Challenger the first man of all men whom Mother Earth had been compelled to recognise.

Only a word by way of epilogue. It is of course well known that the effect of the experiment was a worldwide one. It is true that nowhere did the injured planet emit such a howl as at the actual point of penetration, but she showed that she was indeed one entity by her conduct elsewhere. Through every vent and every volcano she voiced her indignation. Hecla bellowed until the Icelanders feared a cataclysm. Vesuvius blew its head off. Etna spewed up a quantity of lava, and a suit of half-a-million lira damages has been decided against Challenger in the Italian Courts for the destruction of vineyards. Even in Mexico and in the belt of Central America there were signs of intense Plutonic indignation, and the howls of Stromboli filled the whole Eastern Mediterranean. It has been the common ambition of mankind to set the whole world talking. To set the whole world screaming was the privilege of Challenger alone.

We do hope that you have enjoyed reading
this large print book.

Did you know that all of our titles
are available for purchase?

We publish a wide range of high quality
large print books including:
**Romances, Mysteries, Classics**
**General Fiction**
**Non Fiction and Westerns**

Special interest titles available in
large print are:
**The Little Oxford Dictionary**
**Music Book**
**Song Book**
**Hymn Book**
**Service Book**

Also available from us courtesy of Oxford
University Press:
**Young Readers' Dictionary**
**(large print edition)**
**Young Readers' Thesaurus**
**(large print edition)**

For further information or a free
brochure, please contact us at:
**Ulverscroft Large Print Books Ltd.,**
**The Green, Bradgate Road, Anstey,**
**Leicester, LE7 7FU, England.**
**Tel:** (00 44) 0116 236 4325
**Fax:** (00 44) 0116 234 0205

*Other titles published by*
*The House of Ulverscroft:*

## THE LOST WORLD

### Sir Arthur Conan Doyle

This tale of adventure in a fantastic land where 'the ordinary laws of Nature are suspended' has inspired numerous contemporary incarnations, including *Jurassic Park* and *King Kong*. A group of scientists travels to a remote plateau in the Amazon, where time seems to have stood still; their explorations reveal prowling dinosaurs, a war between ape-men and a local tribe, and a sparkling treasure hidden in blue clay. However, when their treacherous guide cuts off their only means of escape, they find themselves stranded in this strange, perilous place that the world has forgotten, forced to defend themselves against some of the fiercest predators that have ever existed . . .

# THE TURN OF THE SCREW

## Henry James

At an isolated stately home in the bleak English countryside, a young governess accepts the job of teaching two beautiful children whose uncle-guardian wants nothing to do with them — and soon she is tormented by visions of ghosts that only she seems able to see: the former governess Miss Jessel and her lover, valet Peter Quint. Even worse, she comes to believe that these ghosts are corrupting the preternaturally angelic souls of little Flora and Miles. The children deny any knowledge of the ghosts, however; and as the tension mounts, the question looms: are the ghosts real, or does the unspoken terror exist only in the governess's mind?

# THE ASPERN PAPERS

## Henry James

1800s Venice is the setting for this tale of greed and obsession: a crumbling, beautiful, mysterious place where the incredible becomes real and the strange is almost commonplace. In fervent pursuit of the letters written by a famous deceased poet to a former lover, the anonymous narrator becomes a lodger under a false name in the dilapidated palazzo of the woman and her spinster niece, in the hope of procuring his prize. The resulting clash of wills and cat-and-mouse games among the trio reveal the deepest motivations that drive human nature — and just how far is the narrator willing to go to get what he wants?

# WHITE FANG

## Jack London

The Yukon, 1800s. A litter of part-dog, part-wolf pups is born in a remote cave; stalked by famine in the harsh environment, White Fang emerges as the only survivor. Quickly learning that the only law of the land is to kill or be killed, the wolf-dog musters the courage and perseverance to endure cruelty and hardship, becoming a savage, morose and solitary fighter. Yet there is one man, a young prospector, who can see beyond White Fang's vicious anger, and decides that it's time to try to win him over . . .